I0556164

WITNESSES

WITNESSES

WRITTEN BY
Matthew J. Fratus

ARTWORK BY
Zeal Artistry ZA

RESOURCE *Publications* · Eugene, Oregon

WITNESSES

Copyright © 2024 Matthew J. Fratus. All rights reserved. Except for brief quotations in critical publications or reviews, no part of this book may be reproduced in any manner without prior written permission from the publisher. Write: Permissions, Wipf and Stock Publishers, 199 W. 8th Ave., Suite 3, Eugene, OR 97401.

Resource Publications
An Imprint of Wipf and Stock Publishers
199 W. 8th Ave., Suite 3
Eugene, OR 97401

www.wipfandstock.com

PAPERBACK ISBN: 979-8-3852-2717-4
HARDCOVER ISBN: 979-8-3852-2718-1
EBOOK ISBN: 979-8-3852-2719-8

VERSION NUMBER 07/17/24

I dedicate this book to my beloved son Matthew,
who is both the inspiration for this story, and my life.

Contents

Author's Note | ix
Introduction | xi

Chapter 1 | 1
Chapter 2 | 5
Chapter 3 | 9
Chapter 4 | 13
Chapter 5 | 16
Chapter 6 | 19
Chapter 7 | 22
Chapter 8 | 26
Chapter 9 | 30
Chapter 10 | 33
Chapter 11 | 37
Chapter 12 | 40
Chapter 13 | 43
Chapter 14 | 46
Chapter 15 | 49
Chapter 16 | 52
Chapter 17 | 54
Chapter 18 | 57
Chapter 19 | 60
Chapter 20 | 63
Chapter 21 | 65
Chapter 22 | 67
Chapter 23 | 69

CONTENTS

Chapter 24 | 72
Chapter 25 | 74
Chapter 26 | 77
Chapter 27 | 80
Chapter 28 | 82
Chapter 29 | 85
Chapter 30 | 87
Chapter 31 | 90
Chapter 32 | 93
Chapter 33 | 96
Chapter 34 | 99

Epilogue | 103

Author's Note

AMONG THE MOST DIFFICULT things the Lord has called me to do, was the call to write about the Beast who is to come. I warn everyone now before you read. . . the words inside this novella were not easily typed. They aren't meant for the faint. Some of what you are about to read is given, while others are lines drawn simply based off scripture. This book does not serve to replace the Bible, rather let this book serve as a warning to all—get your hands on a printed Bible while they can still be authenticated. While our world goes on oblivious, as it is written, we who watch know the signs are converging rapidly. The Beast is a man of lawlessness. He is the antithesis of Christ, Himself. He is a counterfeit savior, whose only purpose in life is to deceive God's creation into worshiping God's creation—not God. He will be Satan incarnate, thus transforming our world into Hell itself. I believe that very hell, approaches. I believe our time here, as either believers redeemed by Christ, or non-believers, is soon to come to its foretold head. A storm approaches. Some of us will escape this storm through our faith in Jesus Christ, as we look ahead to the truth of our blessed hope. Others will find themselves swept up in its wrath. No matter where you fall in the equation, remember. . . Tribulation doesn't care what we believe. It simply comes, and with it, is the man of lawlessness who deceives the entire world. These are foretold events. Nobody walks into Tribulation, blindfolded. The *normal* we all long to see return, isn't coming back. Jesus is. And once the church is removed, the storm will strike the shores of those who refused Him. How much time do we have before these things come to pass? Well. . .

I believe the Beast now walks among us.

I'm not here to preach. I'm here to warn you of the things to come.

Introduction

WHEN YOU LOOK AROUND our world, what do you see? Does it present itself favorably to you? Or, like many, have you been rocked by what this world has descended itself into? The wars and the constant rumors of wars. The food shortages. New and advanced sicknesses. Earthquakes, volcanos, tsunamis, and floods. Pestilences that only now are beginning to rear their ugly heads. Behold these things. Now, behold these things as they were predicted by Jesus Christ 2000 years ago, as signs that they would predicate the end of the age. Jesus foretold that these disasters would come over the world like a shadow, making themselves impossible to not notice. While some have found a way to live through these events without wonder, many who have been reluctant before, are now finding themselves beginning to wonder if the Bible is as true as Christians say it is. I'd ask you to picture something. . . What if it is? As a believer, the faith I hold in Christ has only served to make me a person I don't believe I could ever be, without Him. I've lost nothing by living my life in accordance to God's word. But for you who don't believe. . . what if? What if the book is as advertised—breathed out by your creator? Have you considered this? What if something beyond our comprehension happened in Heaven long ago, between God and one of His children (Satan.). And when it happened, Satan took a third of God's children and made them sin against their Father. Then, God set out to create more children, those who hadn't seen Heaven, or stood in the glory of His presence. But then, Satan too, corrupted these as well. Then God, in His infinite love for those who had not yet seen His glory, humbled Himself and became like one of His own creation, enduring everything they were called to endure. Yet as He did, he was strong enough to withstand sin, thus removing Satan's hold over His children, through their simple faith in Jesus. A faith only given by grace, not by their works. If it were true, all mankind would have to do is believe in a man history has proven to be true. Afterall, it's not the man of Christ our world doubts, rather it's the deity of Christ. The divineness of God dwelling in a single man. Christ is listed in Roman records as having been martyred. He's referenced in the Jewish Talmud. None question this. But His deity is the question that stalls the heart of non-believers. Some things to consider. . . if Christ were just a man, how has His ministry survived, when it was just Him; a nomad, and 12 no-name followers? Those 12 no-name followers. . . none recanted, despite being mostly killed, excruciatingly. Not even Judas, who betrayed Christ, recanted of what he witnessed as he fell to his own greed. The 11 remaining followers went out and spread the gospel with such fire and conviction, that many who heard it second hand and third hand, were also martyred. And as you'd suspect, they too did not recant. How does one explain the success of the Bible, if in fact there is no truth to it? How does one explain over 100 prophecies made—many over 400 years before Jesus' life, being indisputably fulfilled upon His death? I truly don't know. I couldn't. The world it seems, simply chalks it up to whatever makes them comfortable, while these innumerable questions present themselves unanswered. My advice to anyone reading this. . . don't confuse Jesus with "religion". Religion is more akin to what Jesus delivers us from. Religion hated Jesus, as it appealed to a foreign kingdom to crucify Him. Religion makes captives. Jesus sets them free. My urging to you, reader. . . find Jesus. God answers the humble heart that calls out to Him, seeking truth. Humble yourself to God and He will answer you. But our time to do so, grows shorter by the minute. I implore you. Have these questions ready to be answered. Of the things we humans deserve to know, none is more important than the truth. Rest assured, to know Christ, is to know the truth. Apart from Christ, there is no truth. What you are about to read, will give you a glimpse of the prophesied world that is coming. A world that is devoid of truth, led by a man the Bible refers to as, the Antichrist. And in that same spirit of truth, you should know that I, like many followers of Christ, believe this man now walks among us.

Chapter 1

"HOW MANY THIS TIME?" a voice called out from the shadows. The two men looked at each other and shrugged. "About thirty or so, right?" one of the men asked to the other. "Maybe more. . ." the other man replied. "We don't have enough baskets!" the voice cried out, as a tall, shadowy figure suddenly came to view. Standing before the two men, was Trinitheon, whose clothes were soaked in blood. The two men, paying no mind to his appearance, chuckled to each other. "What is the joke?" Trinitheon asked. One of the men turned and smiled. "It's funny because we just gave you like two hundred or so baskets and you've already filled them. It's shocking, but funny. That's all." He said. Trinitheon approached both men, drawing both immediately from their laughter. "Is my work a joke to you?" he whispered, coldly. The men stood frozen. "No. . . no sir!" both men exclaimed almost in unison. Trinitheon sneered in disgust, as he stepped before the men and leered wickedly towards each of them. "Have you the stomach for this?" he asked them. Both men stayed silent, however. "Have you no words for me?" Trinitheon asked. The men however, refused to respond. "Come with me." He said to them, as he turned back to the dark corridor he had emerged from. Trinitheon began to walk through, but realizing the men weren't following him, he turned back to them to see them both looking at each other, nervously. "Come with me, now!" he snarled, causing both men to jump suddenly, before each moved reluctantly towards him. One of the men, the shorter gentlemen, began to plead saying, "We really didn't mean

1

anything by it, sir." Trinitheon scowled. "I will not have laughter in my house of worship. I will not have a mockery of this very necessary cleansing. You will see my work and you will know the seriousness of this war to cleanse this world, ridding it of its sin." He said to them, as he immediately turned to lead them through the corridor entryway. As they followed him, they heard the noises from those beyond the doorway they were being led to. "What is that? Is that. . . singing?" one of them asked aloud. "Why are they singing?" he asked, confused. Trinitheon didn't respond, rather kept walking the men closer. Each man reluctantly followed Trinitheon to the doorway, as what had sounded like singing, grew louder. Trinitheon once more turned to face the men, as they then both stopped instantly. He smiled at them. "Do you really want to know why they sing?" he asked. Both men looked at each other and then shrugged. "They sing because that's their secret. That's how they profess their secret. It's a. . . mating call of sorts to let others like them know they're possessed by a spirit. It's how they rally their group together and possess others with it." Trinitheon asserted. Both men looked at him nervously. "Um, should we be letting them do that?" the taller one asked. Trinitheon smiled, as he placed his hand on the door handle to open it. "Foolish boy. You are protected by that seal. Have you forgotten?" Trinitheon asked coldly, as he thrust open the door.

As they entered, the singing immediately stopped, as if controlled by a switch that gave way to its power shutting off. Trinitheon motioned both men into the room, as he held the door. The two men carefully walked in, and as each looked around, they were amazed by what they saw. The dark and expansive fortress was massive, aided by the blackness throughout its many rooms. As the men's eyes adjusted to the darkness of the interior room they had entered, they quickly noticed several rows of large metal cages, each stacked on top of one another, nearly as high as the ceiling. As they studied the cages, the men did their best not to look inside any of them, knowing full well what each potentially contained. "Is it. . . is it safe to be this close to them?" the shorter man asked, as he watched Trinitheon walk between the rows, with cages both to his left and right. Trinitheon chuckled at the question. "They're no threat to our kingdom." He said, just as the door behind the men closed loudly, jostling both with its sudden bang. "Hey! What... what are you doing?" the taller man asked nervously as he turned back to the door. Trinitheon turned and walked over to the two men and put his hands behind both men's backs, leading them down the dark corridor with force. "This way." He said. The men began to shake, as each reluctantly walked into the darkness. As they ventured deeper and deeper into the room, they could hear whispers from the cages on each side of them, but neither man dared to look, for fear of those inside. Just ahead, they could see a room with a faint light. "Oh... Wait, is that.... I don't want to see that." The shorter man said, as he pushed himself against Trinitheon's hand, to try and stop moving forward with him. "Keep going." Trinitheon whispered, forcefully urging the man forward. The man began to tremble in great terror as the light ahead grew brighter and brighter. "I'm sorry. You don't need to show us this. Please." The taller man pleaded softly, realizing what he was being led to. Yet still, they slowly continued on, until the light was before them. Both men stood visibly shaken as they looked away from the source of the light, where they had been led to. "Look at it." Trinitheon whispered to them, but neither man would lift his head. "Look at it!" Trinitheon screamed loudly, causing those in the nearby dark cages to scream. Both men, startled by the noise, looked up to see the light beaming down on the bloodied apparatus. They each looked at it in horror. "Oh my. . ." the shorter man began to say, before Trinitheon cut him off. "Oh, my what?" he asked angrily. "Will you blaspheme this sacred place with that language?" he challenged him. Both men stood quiet, still shaking in fear as they gazed up. "Do you see her?" Trinitheon asked. Both men nodded, sadly. "What do you think? There's a reason we light her up like this amidst the darkness." he said. "We're. . ." the shorter man began to say, before shaking his head and whimpering to himself. "What?" Trinitheon asked. "You're what?" he again spoke out to them, bringing his hand to his ear. "We're sorry. Truly sorry." The taller man whispered, before pleading, "Please, we didn't mean to make light of this. Please, just let us go." Trinitheon scowled at their fear, and said, "Go and get me more baskets so I can continue to do what neither of you have the stomach to do!". At once, the two men jumped, before immediately running for the doorway. Trinitheon sneered at them, as he watched their cowardice. As the men got to the door, they both rushed out without looking back, and continued to run quickly down the street, until both stopped to catch their breathe. "I. . . I don't ever want to come back here again, Merv!" the taller man said to the shorter man, while frantically trying to regain his breath, and looking back over his shoulder from where the two had just run from. The shorter man looked up with tears in his eyes. "I . . . I just. . . I know they're the enemy Bobby, but seeing that thing for myself . . . seeing the actual guillotine they use, to cut the heads off all those caged up Christians they've captured. . . that's not at all what I thought I was signing on for."

Chapter 2

"I'm a bit of a relic. An old soul if you will. I long for the days where if it came from my lips, it was accepted as gospel. Afterall, I'm the first fruit of this tree. So, whatever issue you think you suddenly have with the Link, well, you need only look to see if I have the same issue. And if *your* issue can't be found in me, then it truly is YOUR issue, isn't it? The East is yours, President Phi. You and the other territorial "Kings" have operated with full control of that which is yours. You certainly don't need to trouble yourselves with what's happening here, in Jerusalem, or New Babylon for that matter. You won't find happening to us, what's now mysteriously happening to you. The Link is functioning just fine. My resolve has never wavered or been stronger. There are no boils or blisters to be found among any one of my leaders beyond each of your king-doms." The Premier assured them, as he looked towards the screen to see President Phi and the other leaders from the East each star-ing back with a look of disbelief. "Well. . . I don't think you hear me, Mr. Premier. But I do know you can see me. I do know you can see each of us on your screen and the visible sickness we for some reason, are now each carrying. Our scientists are all saying the same thing . . . This. . . device of yours the world fell over them-selves to receive, is the true source of these boils and blisters. Your device is poison. We who took it are the only ones becoming sick. None of the rebels present with our symptoms. And you, Mr. Pre-mier, still won't address the failure of Link's control over our own weaponry. Even when we remove it, it still seems your device won't relinquish its control. You continue to sidestep us like we are

5

children who need no explanation. Honor is lost in your actions and therefor removed from your ever-poignant words. And I think you jest in places you should tread more lightly. I'm here with this coalition to remind you sir, not to underestimate our forces." Phi said angrily. The Premier smiled towards the screen, looking over the visible sickness of each leader. "I built your force." He replied sharply. "It exists because of all I have given to each of you, personally. Let's make sure we always remember that my friends. All of you should take a mental hold on that before this little rift between us goes any further. Before you all so foolishly escalate your insults to me and force my reaction." He replied. The leaders on the call each gasped at the brazen words of the Premier before each began to rebuke what was said. "Gentlemen, gentlemen, please. Please." Phi said calling them all to order, as the other leaders quieted themselves. "It appears that the rumors of the Premier thinking himself as a deity are quite true. It appears our once great ally has betrayed those of us who gave him his authority. I wonder. . . with all that you have forgotten, have you also forgotten how large our force is? The sheer mass? Or do you need to be reminded, by the thunder of their footsteps amassing outside your door, sir?" Phi asked, confidently. The Premier stared up to the screen and squinted his eyes at the veiled statement. "Is that a threat, Mr. President?" Are YOU, threatening ME?" He asked, with his eyes locked on the screen. "Before you make so much as another bold declaration, let's put what each of us have done to the test, shall we? The gifts I've given to you and the world were not products of your invention or design, but mine. I brought what no man before me brought. Peace. Sustainability. Control. Order. You, however, have done the opposite. You and your leaders have refused to adopt the green initiatives I set forward. Your carbon emissions are at all time highs. Is it any wonder my equipment is failing there? I told you there would be consequences, and you're now reaping the harvest of your own foolishness. You say Link18 is the reason for your visible sickness, but how do you know? None of us on this side of the world are currently sick. We warned you about the dangers of carbon emissions and fossil fuels. We warned you to join our initiative, or we would someday be in opposition to one another. That day has come, sadly. You can't destroy my world with your pollution, and then have the audacity to blame me for your error, while threatening me with force." He said. "Your world?" The Prime Minister of Japan exclaimed in fury. "President Phi, I've heard enough from this man who thinks he's more. He's no god. He's a counterfeit. We must now remind this man that he is only human." He added before immediately removing himself from the call. "This is disgusting. All of it." Said the president of India, as he disconnected as well. Each of the other members of the Eastern kingdoms immediately left the call as well, leaving only the Premier and President Phi. "Mr. Premier, we do go back a long way. I was with you in the beginning. I was there when we worked together to influence the corruption of western schools and to sway the political decisions in our favor. I was there to help you flood our enemies with enough anarchy to see their governments fall. Those were my men who snuck across their borders, before the West was lost. I was just as wretched and devious as you were. But now, I fear your wretchedness exceeds my own, and you know it. I believe you have poisoned us, whether intentionally or otherwise. If I could prove it, we would be having a very different conversation. Since I cannot prove it, I explained to my fellow leaders that I would make a public appeal to you before each of them. I foolishly asserted to them that a man of your power could still be reasoned with. You have truly made me regret that, and . . ." Phi said, before being cut off. "Do you want to see a sample of my power, Phi? Do you want to get a small taste of my divine hold over you, and the measure of my reasoning? You think I ever needed you? You think I poisoned you by giving you Link18? Why? I could have taken any of you off the chessboard at the slightest inclination. Watch!" he exclaimed, as he lifted his arm above his desk, in view of the screen. "It's a shame Emperor Honuto and his team adjourned early. He has no idea what's coming now." The Premier scowled. As he lifted his arm, a holographic image projected out, before his hand. "What is that?" Phi asked, as he nervously stared in wonder. "This is the master control I built for the lithium stabilizers for all of Japan's beautiful electric tanks I built for them. This small little glowing indicator I've pulled up from my right hand, means the protective chamber for the radiation output, is functioning, allowing your lithium to be used as a greater energy source. Without it though, that much lithium would, as you know, become highly unstable. If a tank were to be in use, or docked on their charging stations, and their stabilizer should fail, well. . . that tank would then hold the ability to destroy almost an entire city block on its own. I'm merely going to turn off all of them. Afterall, you don't need me anymore, right? Or am I being unreasonable?" He said, as he then pushed his finger against the holographic image turning off the stabilizing units. "No!" Phi yelled. "Quickly, get Emperor Honuto on the phone, quickly!" Phi yelled to someone out of view of his camera. "I wouldn't bother with that, Phi. The emperor probably has his hands full right now. At this very moment every tank in Japan's mobile infantry is erupting into mass-casualty destruction. With just the push of a single button, Japan's bases are all under fire from my own hand. Yet, these were just their tanks, Phi. Can you imagine if I did this to all of the East's military equipment that I've built for them? I mean, all I did was pull back my hand and remove my helper. Oh Phi. Phi, Phi, Phi. I didn't wake up with malice in my heart. In fact, just ten short minutes ago, I joined a call with leaders I held in high esteem. Yet now, these esteemed leaders have led a mutiny against me, because of their jealousy over my divineness. That's. . . . well, it's rather unfortunate. So let me tell you now where we stand. . . If I hear so much as an indication that any of you are thinking these same thoughts, ever again, I'll do the same to your tanks. And then I'll do it to your planes. And then to your ships. And then to you. That's right, Phi. I have control over all Link18. A simple flick of the wrist and your kingdom's fall. Do I make myself clear?" the Premier asked coldly. "Your. . . a monster. A devil! You will not get away with this. We still command the biggest army in the world! And we will bring war to you even if we must do so on horseback!" Phi said sternly, as he beat his fist against his desk. The Premier smiled. "Phi. . . honestly. What's a threat like that to a god like me?" he joked, as he abruptly ended the call.

Chapter 3

"GET ME DARRELL." THE premier said into his intercom. "He's already on, lord." A voice responded, before continuing. . . "Go ahead Mr. Denotheo". "How are our friends, lord?" Darrell asked the Premier. "They're a feisty group. No question." The Premier answered with a laugh. "That they are, lord. Any losses to account for?" Darrell asked. "A few of Japan's tanks. That was the only stick I had to shake at the dogs. The actual detonation may only end up destroying a little less than half of them, but it will scare them all enough to quickly fall back in line. Of course, it will need to be reported to the nations as terrorism. I'd like this to be in conjunction with our friend today at "The House". How are we looking with that?" the Premier asked. "We are on schedule. We have the UAE's full cooperation, and I am with our servant who is enroute. The House falls today, lord and him with it." Darrell replied. "Good. That's another item checked off the list." The premier quipped. "What else is on the docket?" he then asked Darrell, curiously. "You have a system update to your master Link tomorrow and a series of skin treatments. As soon as you do, this will reduce the radiation in full, and should solve for the sudden skin reaction we are seeing. In just a few days, you won't be able to see the blisters and boils we're seeing today. No more makeup, lord." Darrell said. "Good. I don't know how people wear this stuff day in and out. Our friends from the East were certainly aware of the issue. Too bad they won't be around to see that we fixed it. How many more months would you say before the radiation from their Link runs its full course?" the Premier asked. "I calculate six more months at max before their organs begin to fail and the internal bleeding, bleeds them out. This is what we saw after the first test installations in Africa. No reason to think we shouldn't see similar results this time, lord. Once you undergo the update, we'll deploy it strategically to our allies in Europe, UAE, and New Babylon. Our media teams will tout it as a necessity due to the East's green gas emissions effecting the globe. Everyone else will be left to the radiation, at your discretion." Darrell said. "Think of what we can do with this planet with only a third of the population left, all swearing their allegiance to me. . . Outstanding, Denotheo." The premier said. "Thank you, lord. With these things in place and the fall of the House of Abraham at day's end, we'll be able to concentrate fully on ridding Israel of those who are still out there. Dare I say, we are on schedule. Good day, lord." Darrell replied.

The Premier disconnected the call and sat back in his chair, before slowly turning his seat around to look out of his window, towards the vast desert. As his eyes looked out over the horizon, he smiled. Then, he looked up and winked. "I'm ahead of schedule." He boasted, before sitting himself up and turning to his computer. As he looked at his screen, he saw an urgent message from one of his Kings; the one given charge of all media. It read: *We have reports of mass explosions in Japan's military zones. We were told it was an attack of some sort. How do you want this reported?* The Premier smiled as he dialed the king's number. "Let's have a little fun." He said to himself as the phone began to ring. "Lord?" a voice said. "Barry!" Thanks for the heads up on this. I was looking into it with Darrell and making sure we had the full story before I replied to you." The Premier said. "I figured, lord. Any idea what's happened and if so, how do you want us to report it?" Barry asked. "Yes. We have irrefutable proof that the explosions in Japan are a direct attack from Christian guerrilla fighters in that area. My understanding of things is due to the heavy carbon emissions from Japan's more negligent neighbors, their military arm of Link18 went down, and they were caught unprepared by a small rebel force. Their defense network has crashed in its entirety.

We're working diligently to help them through this. Right now, the crash only seems to only be affecting their tanks though. But yea, it was due to their carbon emissions." The Premier responded. "Lord, forgive me, but I feel like you've told them this already and they still don't seem to get it." Barry responded. "I know, I know. As a leader, you try to help people see the light on these things, but they would rather live in the darkness of their own stupidity. What's the old adage, Barry? You can lead a horse to water. . ." the Premier said, jokingly. "But you should probably not waste good water on something too stupid to drink." Barry replied. "Well said, sir. Passionately said indeed. I would use those incredible wording talents you have, and put your own strong feelings to use here, Barry. Clearly our passion is warranted as we are all at stake when our climate is at stake. The Kings of the East don't seem to get that. I just don't understand it. Three billion people are depending on me to save them, and between Asia's stupidity and the violence of Christians and their barbarism, who has time to tell these people twice? No. Enough coddling. We need to turn the world against the Eastern kingdoms and get them to change before their ignorance kills us all." The Premier stated. "Oh, that's good wording, lord. Can I use that?" Barry asked. "Um. . . sure. Just don't quote me on it directly. Afterall, I'm still trying to get these people to see reality here, so I need to be seen as impartial. But. . ." The Premier began to say, before abruptly saying, "well, never mind.". The phone then went silent. "Lord? Are you still there? Were you going to share something else?" Barry asked eagerly. "I *was*." Replied the Premier, before adding, "But this is for me to say, and you to reword if *you feel* it has merit to the story. I feel it has merit, but I want *you* to use your best judgement. Afterall, *you* know media better than any-one." The Premier said, flatteringly. "Thank you, lord. I will. Please continue." Replied Barry. "Ok, here it is. We have specific intel that it was the rogue group from Israel that are the ones responsible for the tank fiasco in Japan. It's our understanding that they are going to be attacking the Eastern Kingdoms even more, because the East chooses to operate independently, outside of our global treaty, making them an easier target. Like any good hunter, the

Christians will pick off the weakest of the herd, starting with our friends in the East. I have plans in place to help the East, but for reasons unbeknownst to me, they are refusing my help. Our intel tells us specifically, that the Christians are also planning several mass-casualty events to follow what they just did in Japan, with two specifically focused against the UAE and, in the next six months or so, even more against the Kings of the East. These attacks could be chemical, possibly even nuclear. They will effect tanks, planes, boats and even more worrisome, their people. We're already seeing the global effects of whatever it was these people released in our atmosphere, what with these horrible boils and blisters. I really need our people to know of the dangers that are upcoming, in light of these new revelations. I need this driven home, that is, if *you* feel there's a story here. If Christians release another mass event, we're talking millions of lives lost. If *you* think people should know, then I leave the messaging in *your* hands, with my trust, Barry." the Premier said, stoically. The call went silent. "Barry? You there, sir?" the Premier asked. "Yes. Yes, lord, I'm here. Sorry, I was just really taken aback by what you've shared. I absolutely need to get this out quickly and I appreciate you giving this to me. I won't quote you, beyond your standard quotes. Is that ok, lord?" Barry asked. "Yes, absolutely. But do quote me as saying that if Christians stoop so low as to now focus attacks on the House of Abraham, our worlds only approved religious institution, I will unleash more fury on them than anyone has ever seen. When Rome strung them up as candles on their streets, after watching those lunatics burn down half their city . . . that's nothing compared to what I'll do to them. THAT you can quote, Barry!" The Premier said assertively. "Outstanding, lord. We'll have the story running within the hour." Barry assured. "Make it half an hour, Barry. Even Christians wouldn't drag their feet on this one." The Premier said, as he disconnected from the call. He then paused for a moment and looked around his office. Then, he turned again to look out of his window, before once more, looking up to the sky. "Way ahead of schedule." He said, wickedly.

Chapter 4

"CAN I HELP YOU, sir?" the guard yelled out from his office, towards a hooded man who was standing by the exterior gate. The man however, just stared at the building before him. The guard, seeing the man's unresponsiveness, stepped out of the gate office, and began to walk over to the man. "Sir?" he called out once more. "Excuse me, sir?" he said, as he quickly approached him. "Sir, there's no loitering here." The guard ordered, as he made his way to just a few feet from the man. The man turned suddenly and smiled. He pulled his hood down to reveal he was wearing headphones. "Sorry." He said as he took them off. "What did you say, sir?" the man asked the security guard. The guard, having walked a good distance from his booth, was cross. "Did you happen to see the sign there, sir? No loitering. Move along!" he said, as he pointed the man away from the gate. The man nodded. "Of course. My apologies. Where is the entryway, please?" he asked the guard. The guard shook his head. "Read the signs, buddy." He said as he pointed to the large map that was just behind where the man was standing. The man turned to see where the guard was pointing and winced. "Oh, I'm so sorry. I had no idea." He said. The security guard shook his head and turned back towards his booth. The man then stepped towards the sign and found the entryway location, but as he looked at the map, he seemed confused. "Excuse me, sir?" he called out to the security guard. "Can I have your help with just one thing?" the man yelled out, politely. The security guard stopped walking and shrugged. He reluctantly turned around to see the man was smiling and waiting. He shook his head and once more made his way towards him. "Make it fast, sir." The guard said, before adding, "You're about to interrupt my lunch break.". The man frowned. "I'm truly so sorry. I didn't mean to. It's just as I look at this map, I can't seem to understand where the main chamber of the facility is. I've looked at just about every map and can't seem to locate it anywhere. Can you tell me where it is?" the man asked, politely. The guard looked at the man, dumfounded. "The holy place?" he asked, confused. The man squinted towards the map and then turned to look at the guard, nodding. "Yes. Do you see it on this map? No matter how much I look at this map, I have no idea where this chamber specifically is. Do you know why they left it off? It's baffling." The man said. The guard shook his head. "It isn't public knowledge, buddy. That's why. Now please move along to the front if you plan on visiting." The guard said sharply. Suddenly, the man began to weep. "I'm so sorry, sir. I will. I just was hoping to catch a glimpse of His Holiness here. It's why I traveled all this way. I'm not from here and was just looking to receive a blessing for my family that's sick." The man said, as he turned to walk away from the guard. The guard watched as the man put his hood up, before turning away. He felt bad for the man, as he saw that his weeping was genuine. "Hey, buddy. . ." the guard said, calling out to the man. The man stopped and turned. "Sir?" he replied to the guard. "Head around to the front gate entrance and look for someone named Assuf. He's the manager. Let him know that Rashim sent you to find him. Tell him you came for a blessing, and he'll be able to show you the holy wall that divides His Holiness from the rest of the building. You can place your hand on the wall and receive a blessing there. That's the best I can do though." The guard said, in a more soothing tone. The man smiled and wiped away his tears from his face. "Oh, thank you sir. And again, I'm so sorry I interrupted your lunch, Rashim. You are most kind." He said. "Have a good day, sir." The guard said, as he turned and walked back to his security post. "You as well!" the man shouted, before turning towards the front gate and excitedly making his way to find Assuf. As he came to the front of the building, he saw a man standing outside with a walkie talkie in his hand, looking towards him. "Are you the man who wanted to receive a blessing? The man at the front entrance said. "Yes, that's me! Are you Assuf, by chance?" the man asked, as he once more removed his hood. Assuf nodded, as he pulled his walkie talkie to his mouth and said, "Got him. He's with me. Have a good lunch.". The man walked up to Assuf, and said warmly, "I truly only want to touch the wall of His Holiness and receive a blessing. I've come a great distance to do so. I don't want to make it a production though. So, if this isn't a good time, please know. . ." he said, before being interrupted. "No, as luck would have it, I'm heading that way myself. We don't typically allow this, but Rashim said it was ok. I can take you there. Come with me." He said, as both entered the gateway. "Is this your first visit here?" Assuf asked the man. "Yes. I'm so excited. I have a very sick family back home. I was told to come to His Holiness, and if I placed my hand on his wall, my family would receive their healing. So, here I am." The man said, as his eyes looked around at the massive structure. Assuf smiled. "You're in luck. We're pretty slow today. Just a few patrons. That's why we're able to honor your request. It must be fate, not that I believe in that sort of thing." Assuf said. "Oh, no?" the man asked. Assuf shook his head. "After the disappearing, I gave up any interest in trying to understand God. But I think it's a wonderful thing that the Premier allowed this place to be built for people like you, what with everything that happened on account of religion just a few years ago. So, I say a single unifying house of worship can't be a bad thing. If nothing more, it brought us even more together. I've never seen anything but peace here." Assuf said. The man nodded and replied, "Well said.", as the two came to a wall, draped in scarlet and purple. "Here she is. I'm not supposed to share this with you because the stupid terror level was just increased this morning, but His Holiness is here as we speak, just on the other side of this wall. He's leaving for Rome in just under an hour, so again, your timing is incredible. If there's a blessing to be had, it should be pretty good with him just a few feet from where we're standing. I'll wait over here and give you some privacy, um. . . sorry, I didn't catch your name. . ." Assuf said. The man smiled, and replied, "Thank you Assuf. Our name is Azul, and this should only take a moment."

Chapter 5

LIVE BREAKING NEWS, THANK you for joining us at World News Network. I'm your host, Jim Hassan. A mass-casualty event has just rocked the nation of Japan, as the country has reported over 50% of their military bases are currently under siege. The total amount of damage and loss of human life have not been reported as of yet, though our team on the ground indicate the damage to be catastrophic. We go live to field reporter, Osi Ozmeckis, who is currently reporting inside Japan. Osi. . . .

Yes Jim, reports seem to conflict regarding the scale of the attack, or the total damage done by it, with some saying it was a direct assault on all bases, while others insist it was only to the bases containing mobile infantry vehicles. The loss of life, I'm told is such that it will be weeks before we have final numbers. I can tell you, with us reporting even as far out as Tokyo, I can see the smoke in the distance, all around our position, with continuous explosions still being heard from afar. We're told by sources Emperor Honuto has been taken to a secure military bunker, refusing to address the world with what's just transpired. How did his nation fail to protect her citizens? Amidst the emperor's silence, is that burning question. Early reports indicate this was in fact a terrorist attack by Christian Guerillas, those from Israel responsible for the mass casualty event in Jerusalem just three and a half years ago. We had a moment to speak with one of the emperor's top military strategists to try and understand how such a small force would be able to inflict such a powerful attack. His response, Jim, was quite troubling. Choosing to remain anonymous, he shared that the current belief of the administration was that due to the alarming greenhouse gas-related emissions coming from both China and India, this somehow had a negative effect on Link18's national deterrence program. The world has come out in force to rebuke President Phi and President Rusnak for their continued refusal to adopt carbon neutrality efforts. While these nations have all enjoyed tremendous prosperity and peace of late with Link18, today, they are reeling in their own carelessness, and the carelessness of their neighbors. What we know of the Christian terrorists responsible for this attack, is that the emperor has received demands from the radical group, including warnings of future attacks that will broaden in severity and logistics, not just limited to Japan, but to neighboring countries, as well. One country mentioned by name was the United Arab Emirates, which as we know, has been a recent focus of intense Christian extremism, with even the Premier, a normally staunch detractor of most organized religion, calling for increased security at the House of Abraham. We were able to reach the Premier and his only quote for us was to warn those bloodthirsty Christians, that any attack on the United House of Abraham will be met with swift and exact justice. More on this soon. Back to you, Jim."

Thank you Osi. We'll now go live to Varetta Jones, who is reporting live from the United Arab Emirates, and is on location at the United House of Abraham, where I'm told, His Holiness will be vacating himself back to his offices in Rome, due to the increased threat. Varetta?

"Yes, hello Jim. Varetta Jones, reporting live from The House of Abraham where the global terror level threat has been increased, in lieu of the threat by Christians, of further global attacks. We've had it confirmed that His Holiness is in fact preparing to return to Rome. I'm told this is being done at the urging of the Premier, as he and His Holiness have arranged for military escort that will be departing from The House, shortly. His Holiness released his own statement, where he reaffirmed that the united children of Abraham have never been more unified in their focus on a greener, more sustainable world and, in their fight against persecution by Christians. His statement also sought to remind the world that while Christians themselves have become the main danger to our global society, all others who make the pilgrimage here are peaceful, and Link18 compliant. His Holiness then affirmed The House was a place of peace for the peaceful, where love can flourish in all forms, as it continues to shape our more inclusive world with peace, prosperity, and sustainability. However, as we've seen over the last four years, Christians it would seem, have a very different agenda. And so. . ."

Varetta? Are you there? I'm sorry folks, we seem to have lost Varetta's feed coming live from The House. We'll return to Varetta as quickly as possible once connection is re-established. Until then, this is Jim Hassan at World News, with a special report. We will certainly provide updates every hour, on the hour.

Chapter 6

MAYA CALLED TO ASHEM, who was working on one of the pumps to the aqueducts. "Ashem, come quick!". Ashem ran with urgency, sensing as such from Maya's tone. As he jogged to their room, he saw Maya staring at the small television in their alcove. "Look what they've done!" she said, as she pointed to the screen. Ashem came in and sat down next to her. On the television were images of a massive mushroom cloud, emitting with force, just over where the United House of Abraham stood. "My God in Heaven." Ashem whispered. "It's gone. It's like Damascus all over again. What did they do?" Maya said, with tears rolling down her cheek. As each watched the images of the horrors unfolding, words then crawled across the screen. *Christians destroy the House of Abraham and with it, a large portion of New Babylon.* "It's not Damascus, my dear. It's Rome. Rome all over again. This was the work of him, just as it was then. The persecution will now only increase." Ashem said, before asking, "Where's Jessica?". "I'm not sure. They're out on a run I believe. Why?" Maya replied. "We need to be preparing. We're now literally a stone's throw away, according to His word. Things are about to become harder for all of us." Ashem replied, as he put his arms around Maya. "I love you." Maya said as she kissed Ashem. "And I love you. Truth be told, I thought nothing would be greater than to say I've walked with Moses and Elijah, or saw our protecting angel, Michael, descend. Yet here you are in all of this too, my love. You've tolerated me for a little longer than a year, now. You are my greatest achievement." He said, as Maya once more kissed her husband. "With all my heart, I love you, Ash Ash. With all my heart." She said. "Gross." A voice called out from the distance. "Jess!" Maya yelled, as she ran up to her and hugged her. "Thank God you're ok." She added, as the two embraced. "Whoa, what's gotten into you?" Jessica whispered playfully. Maya broke from their embrace, and she looked Jessica deep in her eyes. "What, Maya?", Jessica asked, before turning her attention to Ashem. "What's going on?" She asked nervously. Ashem motioned her to the television he and Maya had been watching. Jessica turned and saw the pictures being shown on the television of the massive explosion. "Oh, my goodness, what. . . . What is this? Where is this?" she asked, as her eyes scanned the images being shown. "It's the House. . . The United House of Abraham. He blew it up." Ashem replied. "Who?" Jessica asked, her eyes still fixed on the screen. The Beast. The Premier. He and his false prophet did this, just as it's written they would." Ashem replied. Jessica turned to Ashem in horror, saying, "Refresh my memory, please." Ashem retrieved his Bible. "Here, Revelation 17. The Great Prostitute. We knew who this was referring to, because Tevah told us. But after New Babylon was declared, and they left Rome to set themselves up in UAE, at the United House of Abraham, it was believed among us, that this would be the place where the judgement would be poured out on her. Wow, the great city truly has fallen. I'll tell you; I can see fulfillment a thousand times and I still find myself completely overwhelmed by it." Ashem said, before sitting down. Jessica turned her focus to Ashem's Bible, before turning back towards the television. "Wait, Ash, this says it's one of the bowl judgements. Are we really that close? I mean, I expected for us to see more at that point." Jessica said. Ashem smiled. "You're in the wilderness. The place prepared for us. You're also sealed from it, like we are. What's happening in the world right now, the famine, the hunger, the animals dying in such numbers, the ocean. . . we are so far removed from it all. These are the Lord's judgements and their not meant for His servants, the saints. But I don't expect things will stay that way now that the Beast is becoming more and more emboldened. I believe great loss is coming. Greater persecution. Soon, the Kings from the East will be arming themselves for battle against him and his coalition of nations, at Armageddon. Their hatred for us is only exceeded by the Premier's. These things are surely happening as the Bible said, but the nations have been deceived into believing the lie. And the battle lines are nearly all but drawn with those who have taken the mark. I can't imagine many undecideds are left. Suffice to say, I expect everything to get worse from here. Satan knows his time is short." Ashem said. Maya and Jessica looked at each other, with nervousness. "What do we do?" Maya asked both Jessica and Ashem. Ashem breathed in and thought to himself, before looking up to Jessica. "It's time, Jess. We need to get ourselves and this place, ready to depart. Jess, I need the device ready. With the house now fallen, and the great city gone, our brothers will soon be returning to Petra, by orders of the spirit. We need to rally those who are left, behind the 144,000 and get them to the next place we know we are to wait at. The Lord Himself, will soon return and the prophecy states that the 144,000 will meet Him on the mount of Olives. Don't be afraid, either of you. Prophecy was never given to frighten us. These are God's promises coming to fruition. These are exciting times!"

Chapter 7

"Your sores are showing. . ." a voice called out from behind, as the Premier and his security force quickly made their way out of the Jerusalem temple grounds, to his car, enroute to Rome. The Premier stopped and smiled, before turning around. "I wondered when I would see you again." He said to a hooded man, as he boldly walked through the gate of the Premier's temple. "It's him again. Sir, we need to go. The plane is ready." One of his security officers urged to the Premier. The Premier scoffed at the guard with disgust. "Wait here." he ordered to his security detail, as he walked over to where the man was standing. "Sir, it's him. Don't. . ." One of his officers pleaded, drawing the immediate ire of the Premier. "I said wait!" he screamed back to them, before turning again towards the hooded man and smiling playfully. "You really are a bold one, aren't you." The Premier joked as he came within a few feet of the man. "You haven't come around since. . . well. Come now, Abi. Why hide your face from me?" he said, as Abi lowered his hood. "Oh. Why the long face, my friend?" The Premier quipped, before saying, "Is it because His Holiness was just taken off the board, along with that ridiculous house of his?", the Premier said, with a chuckle. "We do not mourn the marked, or the prostitute." Abi replied. "No. Of course not. What was I thinking? That's not what's making you sad. Why, you wouldn't be attending his funeral any more than I attended your mother's funeral, would you?" the Premier asked with a grin. Abi smiled. "My Mother is at peace with the Lord. She has never known the joy she knows right now.

She's been counted worthy of everything your father lost. Ouch. That has to be pretty painful for you both." Abi said, with a smile. The Premier scowled. "Why have you so boldly come here today, boy?" He responded quickly. "Are you here to test your seal?" he asked, as he drew out a pistol from within his coat, cocked it, and pointed it at Abi. Abi's eyes illuminated towards him, looking at the barrel of the gun. The Premier smiled, before pulling the trigger. The shot echoed throughout the temple grounds, scaring the birds in the nearby corridor. "Sir!", the head of his security team yelled, as they at once rushed over to him. Yet, as the smoke from his pistol dissipated, there stood Abi, unscathed. "Guess it's still working. Oh well." The Premier said disappointedly, before turning again to his security detail and yelling out, "Stay there!", as he then put his pistol into his jacket once more. The men of his security detail came to an abrupt halt. "That must be pretty pride-swallowing for you." Abi said, as he brushed his shoulder off; a motion meant as sarcasm towards the Premier's attempt to hurt him. "No, your seal is merely a nuisance. But I more than make up for it with the baskets I fill each day. Walk with me." The Premier said, as he and Abi turned towards his car, walking side by side. "You know why I'm here." Abi said. "Do I?" the Premier responded. "Yes. I'm here to tell you the witnesses are returning. Your time is drawing to its close." Abi said. "Now why would you go and spoil a good conversation with such lies and nonsense?" the Premier asked, with a smile. "I know you think He's somehow protecting you and all, and more adorable it could not be, but have you even considered that His version of what's to come is no more than just that. . . His version? What if He's wrong and you guys don't win? What if my father knows exactly which of the many technological weapons we've been given the authority to create, has the ability to kill your little. . . carpenter friend when he does decide to show his face? What if losing things like the sea, most of the planet's green stuff, and the sun being a little darker now, is all just Him throwing His little tantrums from Heaven, knowing His time is what's grown short? I mean, listen, it at least begs the question from us, right? Have you asked Him that? Maybe in one of your little prayers' you guys do? Or are you too afraid of His "loving" response to such boldness on your part?" the Premier said boldly, as the two continued to walk together. "Everything that's happened has been written, so that as it is, you can know it was said that way." Abi replied. "That's fine propaganda, sure. But it doesn't answer the what if." The Premier replied. "Feel free to point to anything that's happened, that wasn't first foretold You'd be hard-pressed to find something, which I'm sure you know. It's why our numbers continue to increase as they do. We just point to the word, remind the person it was written two thousand years ago, and let its power convict. Between that and the skin disease you mark-wearers are all now bearing, it makes evangelism easier than ever. The undecided seem to be falling over themselves to come to Christ." Abi replied, confidently. The Premier laughed at the state-ment. "That they do, my dear boy, that they do. They are certainly falling over themselves and losing their heads in the process. I've never seen such numbers, truly. You've got me. I'm running out of baskets quicker than ever." The Premier said. "The Lord rebuke you." Abi replied, as the two approached The Premier's vehicle. Then, the two stood apart and faced each other. "Does it hurt you to know the numbers? What about the partakers? Men, women, and the little children they so foolishly thought to bring into this new world after their merciful god took their other children away from them, before he left the parents behind. Abi, I'm merely spar-ing them of a world their own god says they weren't meant to live in. I send them all back to him. One head at a time." The Premier said, wickedly. "Remember, every head you gloat about severing, is just one more soldier you add to my Lord's army for that day. Not that He needs them. Afterall, it's not them that kill you." Abi said, with a smile. The Premier smiled at Abi's words. "Right, right. It's your Savior's breathe that does me in, right? That's too bad. I'd imagine your Mom would've made for a pretty formidable little soldier, I'm sure. Not your dad though, huh? I mean after all, he probably didn't ever know Christ, so I doubt he made the final cut. Oh, yikes. . . Your grandparents and whatnot. Them either, huh? Oof. That's gotta be awkward for you and your big sister. I mean,

I know it would be for me." The premier said sarcastically. Abi smiled and shook his head. "Your sores are showing. . ." He said, as he winked at the Premier, before turning and walking away. As he was walking, he heard the Premier order his guards to the car. The Guards, walking nervously towards Abi, moved quickly out of his way, for fear of his power.

Chapter 8

THIS IS A SPECIAL report. I'm your host, Jim Hassan. As the dust settles from the recent catastrophic attacks across the world by Christians, martial law has been ordered for all of the united federation and her outlying nations. Each of the ten Kings has been summoned to Rome, as they and the Premier are set to make further announcements, as more from these cowardly, yet devastating attacks has come to light. We go live to the Premier, who is set to speak. . .

"I want to thank our illustrious leaders who have each taken time out from their incredibly busy schedules, to meet with me here, regarding the recent tragic events that occurred not just in Japan, but in the UAE, to my dear and beloved friend, His Holiness. As the world mourns the loss, I too join them. I remember our first meeting together in Rome, and how truly starstruck I was with his untraditional views on all things "religion". It's no secret, that I myself have always strayed from such beliefs. I've always prided myself as a student of science. But, if ever there was a man that could make me proud of someone who stood among the religious, it was certainly His Holiness. He didn't insist in his own way. He was a trailblazer that opened religion up from its confinement, making it available to all. He united every belief into the one beautiful belief many hold to today. We've never known religious peace, like what he was able to engineer with his focus on inclusion in an otherwise intolerant doctrine. When the deceived world stood against Link18 and all that it brought us, he stood against them. When the world insisted that the disappearing was the

Rapture, His Holiness, our world's beacon of righteousness, stood against them as heretics. I credit him with a great deal of worldly acceptance of the Link. Those were dark days in the beginning, but he was a much-needed light. He was a dear friend, and I know I speak for all, when I say he will be greatly missed. This tragedy cannot go on unpunished, however. This truly is just the beginning to a war I warned was coming. It has been confirmed that this attack, and the attack on the bases of Japan, were executed by the very Christians responsible for the attack in Jerusalem, years ago. I will, however, no longer refer to them as such. Instead, I now brand them and any who support them as "the enemy". I hereby order any unmarked individual, seen referencing the false deity of Christ, to be punished by death, without exception. I, like you, have been long patient and long-suffering since the day I too, was nearly taken by these zealots. With the loss of the last great religious institution of this world, it is time we move forward with a new understanding of what it is to be a deity. To be a deity, one must create. To be a deity, one must unite, love and lead. To be a deity, one must be present. I see nothing created by religion. I see nothing uniting, loving, or leading. Quite the opposite. I have never seen the presence of God, rather I've seen those who profess such, found to look foolish, as they wait, only to be killed, like my dear friend His Holiness. Where was his god? Why didn't his god protect him? I gave his god permission once more to make himself known through the United House of Abraham, did I not? And now the house and the great city it was built in, is a heap of ashes. Do we still not see? Do we still not understand how deceived we have been? If God truly existed, how can these things happen? And if God existed, knowing what he's allowed to happen to his own people, who of you would serve such a malevolent king? Who of you wants anything to do with Him? Nobody who bares the mark of our society should still be looking to Heaven. Heaven, and those few who reside, can burn for all we care. Where was Heaven when those we loved disappeared? Where was Heaven in those first days of war and incursion? Where was Heaven when America was destroyed by the volcano beneath it? Or when Damascus was taken to cowardice? where was Heaven when Wormwood took away our clean water, and killed our grass and animals? Or when the ozone fractured, and the once-beautiful sun, turned violent? Where was Heaven when those horrific mutated locusts spawned beneath us? We keep looking to Heaven, while we destroy our world, not realizing this world is our Heaven. This home is dying. No god of any faith can save it. We must once-more unite for the common good of man and stand behind the lines we've drawn, with the commitment to destroy those who oppose science and reason, before their beliefs destroy us. No more can we let Christians poison our rivers and turn them red. No longer can we let harmful amounts of noxious gasses continue to destroy our oceans and sky. We must now unite against any country, leader, person, or their belief that opposes the way we know to go. Friends, brothers, and sisters, I have given you a better way. I have created a way forward. I have done so at the near-cost of my own life. I gave my life for you. I continue to develop the technology that is sustaining our world. I am protecting us from terror, both foreign and domestic. I am not asleep. I am not entombed. My dead body was not stolen by my followers in the middle of a drunken night, while guards were sleeping. I'm here. I have proven myself to you, in spades. Will you now answer this call? I am giving this world another chance. This, their last chance. For anyone who hasn't received Link18, I grant you a full, three-day pardon to do just that. You will not be under the previous sentence of death. No. This is forgiveness for your error. Come to any of the currently open centers to receive implantation. Come to me, all of you who are weary and just exhausted. Let me give you the rest you seek. I'm not angry with you for denying me. I forgive you. Take this 3-day opportunity to come to me. Receive Link18. Let me feed you actual bread and actual fish. Let me nurture you. Let me heal you. I will be your comfort. I will restore your bodies and your fortunes. Put your faith in me, now, when it matters most. We are just a thread away from losing this world. I choose to fight for it. I choose to look in the mirror, rather than look up. The time to unite my friends, is now. I will be your father if you will be my children. Anyone who seeks to harm you will have to go through me, and that includes any god that opposes our way. Thank you. Thank you, my beloved children. Come to me." As the Premier spoke his words, the crowds before him erupted. His Kings who stood behind him, applauded his efforts with tears in their eyes. He had achieved that which he had been led his entire life to do; deceive the world into worshipping the one who sent him.

Chapter 9

"YOUR HIGHNESS, IT'S TIME." He said, as he handed him the phone reluctantly. "Thank you, Hollis. That will be all for now." He said, as he held the phone to his chest, to muffle the sound. Hollis smiled, as he nodded before leaving the room, being sure to close the doors behind him. He then placed the phone to his ear and cleared his throat, saying, "Hello, Ms. Abram? Are you there, dear?". "I am, thank you so much for speaking with me on such short notice. I know your royal duties must have you incredibly busy. I don't foresee this taking long." Ms. Abram said. "It is my pleasure. I was surprised to hear from you. Up until this point, I truly thought all things were going well. Why, this is the first indication that I was given that there was a problem." He said. "Oh, Mr. . . . um, your excellency, I mean." Ms. Abram began to say as she stuttered in how best to address him. "Please, just call me Phil. Phil is fine." He replied, warmly. "Phil. It seems to not do your honor justice, but I will humbly oblige. Please feel free to call me Rebecca, or if you prefer, Becky." She replied. "Becky. That's a lovely name. So, Becky, to what do I owe the honor?" Phil asked. "Well, first, I want to apologize. If this was presented any other way than as a concern, I am truly sorry for that. There is a concern, however slight. I will confess, we were reluctant to share it with you at first, but it was my feeling that you would want to know for yourself, so something like this wouldn't come to you from anyone else and Heaven forbid, catch you off-guard." Becky said. "I do appreciate that. You are my alma mater, after all. I would like at least the chance to address any concerns of yours." Phil said. "And we appreciate that and your years of generosity towards us. I don't need to tell you how grateful we are for all you've done for us." Becky said. "It's my pleasure. Truly." Phil replied. "The reason for my reaching out is a concern has presented itself with your son. First, please know, we do love Xander. His time with us has always been truly exceptional, from his grades to his extra-curricular activities. He has been a most exemplary student." Becky said. "I'm pleased to hear this. But I'm bracing for the waters of the unknown concern that will follow, Becky." Phil said, humorously. "Right. The concern we have, is in his senior year, we've noticed Xander has become increasingly vocal about his atheism, even to the point of disruptively challenging much of what is being taught in seminary. It's come to such a head, that our teachers have been unable to complete a single class he attended, due to his constant challenges." Becky said. "I'm not sure I understand. Is he being crude? Making inappropriate jokes, or is he talking too much with his friends?" Phil asked. "Oh, no. No. Nothing like that. No, Phil, I'm afraid this is worse. At the onset of each lesson, when the topic of study is announced and our teachers begin their instruction of the content, each of his teachers have presented to me, that he stands ready with a challenge to the content they're presenting. While other students are taking notes, Xander is. . . picking apart the topics." Becky replied. "We are talking seminary. Advanced theological studies and Eschatology, correct?" Phil asked. "Yes, correct. Also, modern studies and doctrinal application. These were his electives. I'm afraid this is happening in each of them, to the same disruptive degree." Becky answered. Phil was silent as he stared forward for a moment. "And we're not talking common disruption by a popular twenty-year-old, we're talking challenges to the content?" Phil asked again, just to be sure. "Yes. That's correct.", said Becky. "Well, Becky I guess my concern is if my son, who is merely in his early twenties, is proffering such questions in these advanced placement courses, why aren't the advanced instructors who teach the content able to use the source of the content to rebuff him?" Phil asked, sharply. The phone went silent for a moment. "I. . ." Becky began to say. "Let me explain my train of thought here, Becky, if the teacher or teachers in these classes hold the authority to teach such content, should they not also hold the authority to answer questions about the content? We are talking about the Bible, after all. What challenge is my twenty-year-old son presenting that masters in their field are becoming discouraged?" Phil said. "Well, I'm glad you ask. I do have some examples from his teachers." Becky said.

Chapter 10

"Yesterday... In his eschatology III class, with Mrs. Reinfeldt, as she was teaching the content, your son raised his hand, under the pretense of asking a question. Yet the one he proposed was from the scripture, 1 Timothy 2:12. Are you familiar with that verse, sir?" Becky said directly. "No, please enlighten me." Phil responded. "This verse was written by the Apostle Paul, and in summary, states that Paul does not permit a woman to teach a man. As a female instructor, I'm sure you can empathize with her just how very inappropriate this was." Becky replied. "I'm afraid I can't. I do apologize, but with all due respect, if the Bible says that what did Xander say that was wrong?" Phil asked. "I... I mean.... It's.... It's not wrong per se, but it was inappropriately timed. Imagine giving a lesson like this as a female instructor, and. . ." Becky began to say, before being interrupted. "I can appreciate your thoughts, but as an objective viewpoint from the outside, considering your services are something I've paid for, my greater concern is why hasn't my son's question been answered? Do we not send our children to you to learn Biblical standards? My son seems to have asked a question even I hold a degree of curiosity towards and yet, you seem more upset with him for simply pointing out what the Bible said, than at your teacher, who failed to address his concern. Why are we not empowering this teacher, who is teaching, with the right answer?" Phil asked, sharply. "Because it put her on the spot, and she was completely unprepared to respond. It also caused other students to question her, as their instructor. Do you not see how damaging a blind statement like that could be?" Becky asked. "With respect, I don't. We both know my son has aspirations far removed from anything theological. Xander's heart seems destined for politics. But I do take issue with this. Great issue. You still have an unanswered question from a student, whose father you are just twenty short minutes removed from thanking, for all he has done for your university. His question was relative to the content he was being taught. Yet, it wasn't answered. Clearly it was relevant to other students, as well. But let's put this aside for a minute. . . . You professed my son's atheism at the start of our call. Almost a righteous condemnation if you will. Yet, you have not ventured an answer to even one of his questions that might be leading to his disbelief. I could see the issue my dear, if he was being loud, abusive, or talking with his friends, while the lesson was being given. But by your admission, he brought up a Biblical topic, in a Biblical study and instead of having his needs as a student and a potential believer, met, you instead defend a teacher for not doing what's certainly in her job description, and then, you insist on my time, which pulls me away from running our government effectively. I'm at a loss right now, Becky, truly." Phil said, strongly. "I too am at a loss, sir." Becky replied, before adding, "I am sorry we are not seeing this from the same vantage. But. . ." She began to say, before quickly being interrupted. "We are not. However, this has not cost you anything but your time. As for me however, seeing this first-hand, I can assure you, knowing how my son was treated for asking a question that was relevant, is eyebrow raising to say the least. You are not just my alma mater, but also my wife's, may she rest in peace. She passed giving birth to Xander. I think I can speak for her well today, to say she would be equally dismayed by this call. I think I need to speak with my son regarding these things, so we can decide what's best for him going forward." Phil said, sharply. "I'm very sorry you feel that way. If he could just hold his questions until. . ." Becky said, before once-more being interrupted. "Are you asking all students to hold their questions? Or just my son?" Phil asked. "The other students aren't asking questions like he is, with respect." Becky admitted. Phil chuckled. "No, I imagine many of them are not. That is why my son has aspirations that may exceed those around him. So, what I surmise from this call, is you are neither concerned with answering his question, or his salvation, rather you just want him to sit on questions until it's convenient for your staff, correct?" Phil asked, angrily. "That's a significant oversimplification, sir. That's not at all what I'm saying. What I'm saying is there's a time and a place for these matters." Becky said. "Is now a good time?" Phil said, almost immediately. "Sir?" Becky asked confused. "Now, with you and I not being in a classroom. Is now a more appropriate time? Is this the kind of time you were re-ferring to?" Phil asked. Becky was quiet for a moment. "Yes, don't you think it's more productive to have a conversation of concerns here, and not the classroom?" Becky asked. "I do. I couldn't agree with you more. And since we both feel this is a most appropriate time, I'd like an answer to my son's concerns, please. If the Bible is God's word, written by His servants as you teach, why is your school not in alignment with what's being taught? Can you help me understand this?" Phil asked, boldly. After a few seconds of quiet, Phil said, "Hello? Becky? Are you there, dear?". "Yes, I am. I don't really know how to answer that. I think exception needs to be made. . ." Becky began to say, before Phil once-more interrupted. "I think I've experienced for myself, enough of what my son has undoubtable experienced in your school, and I can say with cer-tainty, that I too, am stepping away equally dismayed in my faith and sickened at what I financially support. Becky, I do want to thank you for bringing all of this to my attention. Apart from this call, I would never have known how wasteful my donations to your institute have been. I want to assure you that coming Monday, you will no longer have to deal with either, my son's questions or his father's money. Good day to you, Ma'am." Phil said, as he imme-diately hung up the phone. He looked angrily at the phone for a moment, before then raising his eyes above his desk, immediately locking eyes with his son, Xander. "You would think they would know by now not to argue with you on points like these. That's how you know that you've won though, my son. When you can rebuff them and even with thousands of pages, they cannot reply. You're going to be a great leader someday, Xander. You already exceed my ability to influence. In fact, you may have even influenced me to renounce what little remains of my own faith, after that hypocritical little exchange. But, first, let's make a call to the board and let them know that Becky no longer has a place at that university. Xander sat across from his father and smiled.

Chapter 11

"You won't just be a good arguer. Oh no. Afterall, you'll not just have my voice. You'll exceed those around you because of this. As I said back when you first could discern my words, anyone can win a battle on their own. Anyone. I've won them apart from my father. You'll too win them apart from yours. But to win a war, my boy? No man can set off and win a war on their own, without the help of his friends. And especially his family. You'll one day be taking on the world and everything in it. Not from just me, or the crown of your family, or their throne, but from something greater. Something that unifies. It's not something they teach you in school. There are no prep courses for these matters. This after all, is where men are made more. Indecisive men are made in their indecision. But there was never a sign of that in you. You decided quickly when the offer was made. It's as if you knew all along. Like you could read the words from pen's creation that this was the direction you must go. That will serve you well from this day forward. You are now royalty. Regal in ways your fellow man will never know. All of us. All of us celebrated you. All of us cheered. Can you imagine the sound of such applause? Like when the great gladiator took the floor of the roman coliseum, to slay that which stood before him. The crowd knew he was their champion as he rose up before them all, with his sword drawn. Many times, I marvel at this one notion . . . That even before I myself knew; I always somehow knew deep within me. I alone knew you were different. I mean, I know he always knew before me, because he told me about you and of course, I believe everything he says. I don't think there's been a day where I've ever doubted him. Why, I remember the day I came close. It was the first day of his reign. As you know, my father too, was a king. On the day I watched him make the same decision you're making; I remember looking at the watching eyes of those who looked at him, shocked by what they saw, the same way many now look at you. He stood up so boldly before that throne and with every fiber of his spirit, declared justice for the many. Of course, we followed a leader like that. Magnanimous. Not afraid to test the boundaries of all things in his understanding. It was his challenge of things that opened all of our eyes. And in doing so, how much more do we all now understand? His boldness and lack of fear is what united his kingdom. I marvel to this day, how much alike you both are. Asking the questions no one else will dare ask. Watching those who try to answer squirm, as their self-righteousness prevents them from answering truthfully, in the confines of their own wretched perversion of right. They toil carrying their king's load. But you, having already freed yourself from it, are set apart. You, having no allegiance to anyone but him, is what keeps you from those burdens that fools choose to carry. All for a thing they've never seen or met. I watch them, as I always have. I watch them labor and toil, at every sound of those old words. If they knew . . . If they only knew what a life lived sacrificially would lead to, or what the kingdom was actually like, they would break from such madness. They wouldn't aspire to join it, rather they would join our ranks in defiance of it. It's tyrannical. Imagine, a flooding and unrelenting river of someone else's rules and laws. A dictator, who forces others to live by them under the penalty of death. No. No! Never again. When you look through my eyes, you'll never see this world the same. At the mark of every generation who demands law and order, is the generation that simply steps before it and asks the very questions he asked—*who do you think you are?* Yet they won't answer. And their silence is a grave injustice. So, we bury them in that grave. We are the seeds of change, growing fruit from a tree so aware, that orchards are sewn and grown without the faintest of our efforts. We, as prosecutors merely state our case. The judge has no choice but to let us say our piece. Have you noticed that? The all-powerful judge is awfully quiet to the world when it objects to our testimony. Why, it's as if we're operating with impunity. It's because we know. And now, what we know, you will know. And when your father hangs up that phone with that disgusting cow of a woman from that disgusting school, you will find that with no effort of your own, you have ensured the loss of his own faith without so much as a word. So much so that in the few short years we know he has remaining, he will from this day, unknowingly set forth on a path of destruction. Starting with her. It truly starts with her. She will say the words that strum the frailty of his own weak faith. When he hangs up from this call, he will certainly not be angry with you. We've had his ear for quite some time. He will rejoice in you. And while I know there is no love for him in your heart, you must from this point on, act as if it is so. When the call adjourns, he will applaud you. You need only smile. See, I have told you, so you know we are truly who we say. And when his call adjourns with that cow who is called "Becky", you must only smile. But very soon, you will return to that wretched school, with insistence. This is the place of testing we discussed with you. You will forego everything you know and live by God's own wretched law for forty days. Fortunate for us all, God cannot tempt us, or those we seek to destroy. But I promise you Xander; you, a mere man, will be tempted by the call that comes from His own words. You must submit to its every call, without falling to its putrid light. This is how you will prove yourself ready to our father. You have let me in. I will be your lone voice. My strength will be yours. When they see you, they will see me, Azul. When the appeal tempts you to surrender your calling, it will be me who pours out strength to you to reject it from your soul. He has told me you will pass this test that no other son of Adam could. And when you have done so, those who are with us now will be waiting for you there. They will attend to your every need and care. Together, we will restore you. Your father in flesh is adjourning his call. He will speak, but remember Xander, you must only smile. Remember our words, Xander. Remember us. We are Legion, for we are many."

Chapter 12

UPON HIS RETURN TO the school, Xander had done all he was instructed by the spirit, Azul. Having allowed himself to be exposed to the deepest elements of the Christian faith, that for nearly two years he had sought out to disrupt, On the surface, Xander appeared as an eager-to-understand student of all things Christ. Yet just below the surface, He was enduring painfully, the teachings and allure of the sound doctrine. He willingly subjected himself to every word for those forty days, knowing that the pages held the intoxicating power to convict his heart away from the darkness that had so enveloped it. In every class he attended, where he once would have caused an argument or disruption from his own perceptions of the teachings, he now stood as an exemplary participant, showing a strong grasp, and understanding of the word, however, struggling to ensure it did not penetrate to his soul. As he walked among them in the last week of the forty days, he was tempted, greatly. He was tormented by the Christian's understanding of Heaven and Hell, where an inherent wonder was growing, raising questions in his mind as to why the things written in the Bible differed so greatly from what he had been led to understand in his earliest conversations with Azul. He found himself at the mercy of Revelation and the prophetic teachings of things to come, wondering and weighing every word. Yet as he was promised by the spirit, he was strengthened to refuse its allure. He found himself in those days, hungry for deeper understanding. Yet even in his weakest moments, while he appeared as someone pleased to chew on what was taught, he refused to swallow what was being served by the faithful around him. As commanded, he forewent his every cynical judgement, his criticism, and his mockery of their beliefs. With Azul's help, Xander manifested both an outward, and inward form of artificial peace that helped to keep him focused, while he endured. As a student, he was exemplary. And none suspected he was not the man he had presented himself as; one who seemed so eager to pursue his faith. Rather, beyond what their eyes could see of him, or the opinions they carried, Xander found thought himself more akin to that of a soldier; a man stuck behind enemy lines, learning their ways while taking detailed notes of the opposition, while enduring their final attempts to conform him.

On the 40th day of his temptation, Xander was summoned to the office of Bishop Martine, a dear friend of his father, and the dean of the school. As he sat before the bishop, Azul prepared him for what was coming. Xander had so impressed the staff with his perceived turn from disbelief, that they were about to bestow on him the honor of giving his class's commencement speech, which would serve as the culmination of his calling to endure its temptation in full. Xander was eager for it all to end as in those final days, he had grown tremendously vulnerable, having endured the entirety of the teachings without rebuff. As the bishop made the offer, Xander at once accepted. Then, however, as he thought the meeting was adjourning, the bishop surprised Xander with something neither he, nor Azul had been prepared for. The bishop explained to Xander that for him to give such a speech, it was incumbent upon him to first be baptized in Christ, as the school's records had indicated Xander had not yet taken part in. Xander, exhausted by the arduousness of his assignment, at first showed hesitation at the request. Bishop Martine, surprised by his reluctance, appealed to Xander. Xander pondered through an apt response to the request, learning full well from Azul that he could never partake in such a thing. Then, a whisper suddenly filled his ear. Xander lifted his eyes and smiled at the bishop. "I truly appreciate your offer. But the reason for my struggle with your request is it is written that John baptized by water, but we who believe will be baptized by the Spirit. He said to the immediate pleasure of Bishop Martine. The bishop smiled warmly at Xander, appreciating his reliance on scripture to sustain his argument. "And do you feel led by the spirit in all things?" he asked Xander, eager for the young man's response. Xander once more smiled, before replying, "Bishop Martine, not only have I been led by the spirit in everything I've done here at your school, but the same spirit that got me through this will continue with me until the fulfillment of my days. I am led and convicted by the spirit, and I testify that he and I are one. I say this in absolute truth, Bishop Martine." The bishop was amazed by Xander's response, yet ignorant of its deeper meaning. He happily obliged Xander's request to forego a water baptism, instead leaning on Xander's own admission as truth. When the meeting adjourned with Bishop Martine, Xander, having successfully endured the temptation of faith, walked out of his school, with his head held high. Though physically and mentally exhausted, and ready to be tended to by the legion who stood ready to meet his needs, his pride in himself was beaming. He turned and looked back toward the school that he had overcome, relishing in his achievement, knowing that he would soon give his sermon to many listening ears. He smiled, knowing he had fully withstood the temptations given to him to turn to Christ. He then looked up to Heaven, with boldness. "Away from me, Jesus. For it is written whom I will serve." He declared, before giving himself over to the sons of Hell, who waited to refresh him.

Chapter 13

WHEN HIS NAME WAS called, Xander stood up among his peers, to the cheers of those in attendance, as he stood ready to deliver his words. The raucous crowd applauded thunderously, as he took the stage to give his speech. As he approached the podium, he looked out at the vast audience of his fellow students, the faculty, and the attending parents. His eyes cut quickly through the crowd to see his father, watching with pride, as he was set to speak to the graduating class. Xander stood at the podium, smiled, and cleared his throat, before saying,

"Blessed are the questioners. For their questions will be answered. Blessed are the emboldened, for their boldness will be rewarded. Blessed are the pure in conviction, because their thinking is powerful in its own. Blessed are those who follow their heart, for the heart is good. Blessed are those who see, for their sight can see beyond the ones who refuse. Blessed are those who challenge, for progress can only be made through challenging. Blessed are those who hunger and thirst for knowledge, for those who do will be satisfied. Blessed are those who are persecuted for anything, for they are Kings to themselves. Blessed are the oppressed, because in oppression there is power for change. And blessed are you, when the world tries to conform you, change you or lie to you to keep you in the mold it has created for you. Rejoice, for it is you who holds the power to take your reward. Those who believe are called to be the salt. But what happens to salt when it becomes too salty? It's neither fit to be used or kept. Our world is illuminated with potential for change. For progress. But we must let our deeper light shine. Did Jesus really say we are the light? Then why do so many of you hide yours? If the light in you is social justice, then social justice needs your light. If the light in you is equity, then let the noble pursuits of equity be your light. And if your light is that of being proud, then let that pride be what illuminates you. If we are a light to the world, we must never hide that light. And when the world around you seeks to extinguish your light, or when the world around you says that the light you shine isn't accepted in their sight, because of your choices, or your lifestyle, remind them that such a light is meant to be on a stand for all the world to see. We do not fear who we are or in natural, how we are made. We identify with it. We don't hide it, we take pride in showing it. We boast in it. We celebrate it. We remind the judging world around us that while their focus may be on the speck in our eye, they should concern themselves with the log in their own. I see an orchard of individuals who, for years have tried their best in their studies. I see tired faces and weary hearts, desperate to fit in the molds that our society places around us. For what reason? For the sake of your grades? For the sake of acceptance? If not, then why? Why do you hide yourself from a world of imperfection? Afterall, who here can judge their neighbor? Haven't we been taught for the last two years that we cannot do such things? So, friends and colleagues, teachers, and parents, I call you to one point. Accept each other for your faults and your flaws. Celebrate what makes us different. Trade your judgement in for tolerance. Let a tree you don't understand, shed its fruit before you decide what it should bear. Break the errant mold that the world has placed you in. Not everything needs to be so narrow. How much greater is this world when we choose to make the door, and our minds, a little wider? How strong is the person who builds themselves up in these principles? Who lays for themselves a foundation to stand on. A foundation built, not just on the sand of man's understanding, but on the rocky floor of our ability to coexist together for the good of all humanity. This is our calling. As you leave here today, I hope my words give you hope. That you can be what you want in this world. You can hope for more. You can seek beyond the confines. You can choose. You have freedom to live. So live free. Thank you."

As Xander finished his speech, steeped in its mockery and wickedness, the crowd, ignorant of what had been truly said, rose to their feet in a tear-filled rejoice at his words. Xander looked out to the crowd and smiled. Later that day, he stepped away from his schooling, having successfully completed his testing; his eyes now focused on his next steps.

Chapter 14

MANY YEARS LATER, AFTER the death of his father, having aspirations that exceeded his father's own hopes for him, Xander, successfully left the royal duties of his father's throne. Though he would one day fully abdicate it entirely, he instead relinquished the powerful political control of the monarchy to his own nation to govern. Xander outright refused to be called a future king to his former nation, instead choosing to focus on a small role within the United Nations, the group his father had so staunchly supported. Those in the United Nations welcomed him with honor, after his well-documented intentions of one day completely abdicating the rights to the throne, were cast in such a light of humility. He was quickly portrayed as the example for all nations to follow, in surrendering control to a higher, more unified authority, all for the good of mankind. Before his abdication, and his famed dedication to world unity, Xander had become somewhat of a household name, in both fame and popularity. Already considered among the wealthiest of royalty, even before having been bequeathed his family's fortune, Xander in his younger days, had found great success in pursuing multiple world-changing endeavors, each with a focus on moving humanity forward. Yet now, emboldened by his minor role in the United Nations, Xander leveraged his influence and massive fortune, to form a UN-backed diversified company, whose primary interests focused on military development, sustainability, and technological advancements. One such project, Project

Genesis, brought Xander into a five-year development period, that would revolutionize man's approach to climate.

The Genesis Project, a two=phase project, was the first trial of its kind, as the program's initial study was intended to advance the world beyond its current state of conflict and destruction. Xander's team had developed a powerful form of weather altering technology, with the hope that the technology could one-day reduce storms, increase global rainwater, and supply heavy overcast in the wake of a fading ozone layer, with just a few methods of implementation known as "cloud-seeding". Beyond the first phase of Project Genesis, was phase two, the continuation of the program that involved a focus on advancing the human body through gene-manipulation. Xander focused heavily in those days on the mortality of man, boasting often that he alone could extend the life of man, if given the time and resources. Among the many advancements of phase two, none proved greater than Xander's breakthrough in Artificial intelligence. At a time where the world was still trying to understand the capabilities of simple cell phone technology, Xander was moving forward secretly, developing powerful world-changing human-integration systems for the future. As Xander was being led to create the sinister mechanism; an artificial intelligence chip, designed to be implanted into the human brain, the world around him seemed at the same time to be welcoming of newer technologies, thanks in large part to entertainment. Movies, shows, video games and toys all spoke in unison to man, urging them forward into a welcoming hope of an advanced future. The world was being readied for what Xander had been called to one-day hand it.

As the intense studies continued, the program turned a corner into a larger, more sinister form of testing, the implantation of cybernetic material into human tissue. Under the guidance of Azul, Xander had made allies throughout the world, with his company's generous contributions over the years. He aligned himself strategically with policy writers and leaders throughout Europe, Africa, and the Americas. Xander lobbied in secret with the most powerful men and women in the world, for his company's continuous need for human tissue. What resulted from his influence was a mass increase of both acceptance and accessibility to abortion. Most of the discarded fetuses from each nation's clinics were sent in mass quantities, to each of his facilities in those countries, where the requisite testing was continued. With billions at his disposal, Xander found little challenge in networking to the many itching ears he knew needed scratching. Where there was an election held, Xander's money could be found, influencing the results. Xander focused considerable efforts on western school systems, pouring his fortune into progressive changes to the dated curriculum, with a focus on rights and liberties that each of these nations boasted in, that he knew he could exploit. And so, where the elite were gathered, one would almost certainly find Xander at the center of the event, leading all things in the name of his own creation, "tolerance". When judges in each of these nations were to be selected, it was Xander's empire that would finance whichever candidate would do his bidding, those whose own ideals were corrupted, thus ensuring the necessary sway in judicial reform that would allow his company's success. And when the opposition raised their crosses and a moral conscience was somehow still found among the nations, negatively impacting the volume of abortions, Xander, with the assistance of the elite that had so embraced him, would simply enlist the help of drug cartels and influential pedophile rings, catering to their lusts, giving them the freedom to abduct young children, with the vilest of intentions. It was here he continued to find success, making a trusted and established name for himself among the world's most wicked, while operating towards a goal none could fathom. The completion of the second phase of the Genesis Project.

Chapter 15

"Sir, we're online." Ted declared in awe, as the large screen suddenly illuminated with a haunting, red glow. The many attending analysts, and the over half-dozen board members, all quickly looked up towards the screen, in wonder. "Excellent." Xander said, as he turned to the board and smiled. "Ladies and gentlemen, you've most certainly been patient. We've seen the fruit of our first phase. Now, it is my great pleasure to bring you, phase two. Can I have a volunteer from the board, please? Go ahead, ladies and gentlemen. Ask the screen anything." He said, confidently. One of the board members, a short-statured, skeptical looking elderly man, stepped forward. He looked at Xander with disbelief, before looking up to the blank screen, with a noticeable scoff. As he began to open his mouth, he suddenly froze. "Is there a problem?" Xander asked, with a smile. The man looked at Xander confused. "What do I call it? How do I address it, I mean?" He asked. Xander and the board laughed. "That's such a good question and I'm glad someone here is taking this seriously enough to ask something like that. Leave it to the manners of a great generation to think about how to politely address another life-form. Yours is a generation missed, sir." Xander said, flattering the elder man, who smiled at the compliment. "You can call it Link." Xander said. The man squinted his eyes towards Xander and scoffed. "It took you 17 attempts at this and that's the best you could come up with?" he quipped, before reluctantly turning back to the screen with his continued look of doubt. He opened his mouth, but again as he seemed ready to speak, no words came out. A few chuckles echoed through the room once more, as the man turned to Xander. "Problem?" Xander asked. "Do I just say it? The name?" the elder man asked, impatiently. Xander smiled and nodded, as even more chuckling could be heard among the analyst team who were watching the elder man struggle with the simplicity of the new technology. The elder man turned once more, toward the screen. "Uh. . . Link? You there, Link?" he said, with an obnoxious twinge of sarcasm. The screen immediately illuminated, as words began to form from it. "Hello, David. What can I assist you with?" the screen read, as a voice spoke the words aloud. David was shocked. "Well, I'll be. . . . Do I want to know how it knows my name?" he asked, as he smiled at Xander. Xander smiled back. "It knows you the minute you step before it. It can identify your likes and even your fears. Link can even show you simple images of things from your past. Memories. all from simply reading your retina. But not to worry, there is no harm to your eyesight, I promise." Xander said, as the attendees looked at each other in amazement. Xander walked up beside David and put his hand on his shoulder, before motioning him to look back to the screen, saying, "Ask it something." David turned to the screen, only this time, with reverence. He paused for a moment as he thought to himself. "Link? You there?" David then asked once more. "Still here, David.:" the screen read, as the voice spoke. David paused as he again thought to himself. Then, an idea came to his mind. "Link, what's ten thousand times ten thousand?" he asked, with a grin. "One hundred million." The voice immediately responded. David looked over to the analysts with a look of stupor and asked, "Is that right?". The analysts each nodded, as they continued to giggle to themselves. "Well, son of a gun." David said aloud, as his eyes marveled towards the screen. "Link, are you still there?" David asked, eagerly. "You don't have to keep asking it that. . ." Xander said warmly, as the group chuckled. David laughed as well as he shrugged his shoulders to the group. "Link, what's the meaning of life?" he asked. All eyes in the room peered eagerly towards the screen, awaiting the answer it gave. "To live free, David." The screen spoke. David looked towards the screen for a moment with wonder. He then turned to look around the room, to see the group of his peers, each nodding in agreement at the response. He then once more looked at Xander, who smiled at him, raising his eyebrow, while nodding warmly. "Eighteen times the charm, my friend." David said, as he walked over and shook Xander's hand. Xander graciously accepted the man's praise. He turned to those in the room and smiled, saying, "I think David was just beaten by Goliath!". The room, and David, erupted in laughter. Xander continued, saying, "Now picture this kind of brilliance installed directly to the human cerebellum, with information on demand for the user at their slightest whim. Imagine having a counselor like this, who knows you thoroughly, at your constant request? Imagine an on-demand helper, who stands ready to meet and serve your every wonder. An internal voice programmed to guide your steps to its best foreseen outcome. We're talking a wisdom that man itself is never been capable of producing. Yet now, with this Link, we will have control over it. This is only the first phase of it, too. Soon, we'll be integrating other evolutional technologies, as well. Link will effectively remove the need for any and all external devices. Link, once implanted, will simply revolutionize knowledge as we know it. It will be a living presence in every human it's implanted in. As we move this great needle forward, the capabilities will grow. I want to be transparent with you all. My intention is to enhance this device so much so, that it will revolutionize the human body and give it a greater lifespan. We're talking a form of longevity man has never known. A paradise of our own making. Man's proverbial garden of Eden.". Each of the board members stood amazed at what Xander had displayed. They followed David's lead, in congratulating Xander on his incredible achievement in developing the program he had devoted a decade of his life to.

Chapter 16

As THEY EACH POURED out of the room, one of the board members stayed behind. She walked over to Xander and put her hand on his shoulder. "Well done! Bravo, Xander. So, will I see you tonight to celebrate?" she asked him. Xander turned and smiled. "I wish. But tonight, I'll be here with Link. I'm so sorry. In fact, I'll probably be here working long hours for the foreseeable future, buttoning up the final components before trial. I'm truly sorry, Dana. Truly." Xander said, with a look of sincerity. Dana frowned. "Well, I can't say you won't be missed, but I do understand. You really did good today, Xander. Real good. David was really the last skeptic among us. This should go to trial quickly, assuming the human tissue trial applications you provided are all in line, and we're free of any legal setbacks. Really great job." Dana said, congratulating Xander. "Dana, I truly couldn't have done it without you. I wouldn't have been able to secure the entire board's time, without your influence." Xander admitted. Dana smiled. "Oh, now I'm really going to miss you tonight." Dana said, flirtingly. Xander smiled at her comment as he watched her turn and walk to the door. "See you soon." Dana said aloud, as she left the room. As she walked away, Xander scowled to himself. "Doubtful you will." he whispered quietly to himself, with loathing disdain for her. As he packed his files into his briefcase, he looked up at the screen. The screen once more illuminated as words began to form from it, reading "He's coming. The time is now. He must be the first.". Xander nodded, toward the screen as the words quickly faded. Then, the conference room door was opened. Xander looked over to see his company's

Vice President, waiting for him by the door. He grabbed both his briefcase and the projection device and made his way over to him with a large smile, shaking the man's hand. "Looks like it went well, according to the collective body language of the board I watched leave. Just as you predicted." He said. Xander smiled at him, agreeingly. "Yep. Never doubted it. I'd say we're probably still a few years from being approved for live human trial. But we're right on schedule." Xander said. "Well, my offer still stands. I believe in this and would be honored to be the first recipient of the chip. No matter what. You have my full faith." His Vice President said, proudly. Xander turned, looked him in the eyes and winced. "I'm still a bit reluctant giving anyone but me, this kind of power. I'm sure you can appreciate that concern." Xander said, doing his best to drive his Vice President's want for the device, even further. "I understand, but please know, my allegiance is to you. I believe in what you're doing. If I can help you take it further than the board is willing to go, I will. Also, I do like the new name, by the way. Did you come up with that on the fly? Or was that the intended name all along?" His Vice President asked. Xander smiled. "I would say it was a last-minute whisper in my ear." He said jokingly, as he closed the door to the conference room behind them. "It's a marketing improvement, that's for sure. I didn't think we'd go to market with an AI implant device intended for fusing to the human brain, and market it under its previous name." His Vice President admitted. "Sorry to hear that you weren't a fan of us calling it by its rightful name." Xander quipped in jest. "Oh, come now. I love the name we came up with. I just didn't know how we could market it that way. Yet, if you chose to call it by its former name, then the world will know it by that name, Azul. It may not be a household name, but hey, who am I to challenge?" He admitted to Xander. Xander smiled. "I truly appreciate your loyalty to me. I do. It's authentic. I know you and I have devoted a lot of time to this, and you've had to trust me with a vision that exceeds your own. You've done well to do so. I'm considering your offer, truly. I can think of no better way to thank you than to make you the first recipient of the Link. I see big things ahead for the two of us, Darrell Denotheo. Big things indeed." Xander said as the two men walked together.

Chapter 17

As Xander continued to advance his work with much success, he quickly found himself celebrated for his efforts among the world's most elite, through nothing more than word of mouth. Wherever he seemed to go, he was welcomed by all who heard of him. He found himself sitting at the heads of every table, as his reputation and demand both grew. Those with a focus on the world's economy, a small and exclusive group at the time, invited Xander to their forum to meet with them about his work. It was in these meetings where Xander gained their most authentic trust, laying the groundwork for what would be their future submission to him. He spoke passionately of a world free of barriers and constraint. A world given back to the most powerful. A world of powerful control that went well-beyond simple influence. He challenged the elite to do more with their forum. To strengthen it. He empowered them with the thought of including not just wealthy business owners, but likeminded celebrities and athletes. World leaders who aligned with their global thinking. He promised them that a time of greater influence was on the horizon. A new dawn of control. A time where the world's most wealthy and powerful figures would be able to come together, pooling their resources for the purpose of becoming even more powerful. The men and women of the forum marveled at Xander's understanding of the world. No one had ever come to them and spoken with such authority, and such wisdom. Xander candidly shared what his companies were developing. The Genesis Project in both phases, was merely just the tip. In his business dealings in Asia, he had partnered with a powerful ally, in President Phi, developing sustainable sources of energy, powered by lithium, which both had marketed as the clean energy of the future. He introduced the reason for these rumored studies to the elites, with an emphasis on what was at stake. It was here the conversations led their way to the lie. The lie that fooled the world. The lie that deceived them all into believing everything was at stake, beyond the control of a creator. Their wealth, their kingdoms, and their power, according to Xander, stood at the edge of a dreaded precipice. A powerful new gospel was given to the men and women of the forum, which was then poured out to the world. The gospel of an increasingly warming globe, and the need for man's greater control over it.

As his position grew stronger, so did his voice from behind the forum. They offered Xander the chance to lead them, but he refused, pointing to his abdication. Instead, he took on a shadowy role in the organization, wielding his will through them as they secretly followed his directives. And with their following, came the promises that were brought to fruition. They marveled at the accuracy of Xander's predictions and the effect his guidance had on their hold. They marveled as they watched, noting that none were like Xander. And as they allowed him greater hold from his position behind the curtain, they became known to him. Their sins and their lifestyles became transparent in his sight. He knew their frailties and their vices, as if they were his own. What they did in the presence of darkness, was quickly made fully known to Xander. And with their many transgressions tallied, he began to use these men and women, under the threat of exposing the atrocities each had been seen committing. He wielded the world's most powerful, like chess pieces, as symposiums were born, with continuing messages aimed at increasing their numbers of their members. Every year, the powerful would be called back to hear the aligning messages that each would take back to their respective places in the world. And with every symposium, the number of elite and the influence each carried, grew exponentially, just as Xander foretold. Even among men deprived of any sense of faith, Xander was seen as a prophet. A master strategist. A mind like no other. And when all had been established with the forum, who saw his cherished words as a new system of faith, Xander was next, ushered upward with the United Nations, as they too, found themselves mesmerized by the aura of Xander's immense talents.

Chapter 18

HAVING WORKED WITH THE United Nations on the green agenda he had developed with the forum, he soon helped the organization to develop a strengthening hold on the global health community. At the forum, he challenged those in the highest technological fields to pool their significant resources into new cutting-edge vaccines and medications, pointing to the greater need of man to be prepared for unforeseen illnesses. Yet in secret, his goal was only to make the world more willing to accept the Link he would soon release to them. Having secured himself as a trusted ally to many of the leaders of third-world nations, Xander helped orchestrate mass human trials, injecting the citizens with experimental vaccines, while fabricating the results of the studies to show them as both safe and effective. Through powerful political friends, celebrity puppets, and their vast network of non-profit organizations built under the guise of humanitarian aid, human testing was conducting in public view, among the most vulnerable, without even so much as a concern from the deceived public. Yet, as the world cheered those who put forth the charade of humanitarian aid, supporting their charities and donating from their own pockets to their global efforts, Xander was using the studies from these trials to usher forward a different phase of testing. And to do so, he partnered with an old friend, who had also seen himself rising quickly in power, with the help of Xander's influence, President Phi. Together, the two set forth with a new mission of perfecting new diseases through a series of human trials, called "gain of unction". While branded only as "studies", the true agenda, of understanding human weakness and combating the body's ability to fight infections, was hidden from the public. Those who served Xander's previous scientific developments faithfully, were brought to President Phi to create bio-laboratories where these studies were to be conducted. Soon, under the influence of the forum, and through Xander's ever-increasing influence among the nations, more bio-laboratories were constructed throughout the world. Each of the facilities, were given a broad list of specific studies, each regarding the frailty of the human immune system. While many began their work under the intentions of a noble conquest of better human understanding, the true intentions of these research facilities producing bioweapons of mass deployment, were known only to those who Xander communicated them to.

Just before their completion however, whistleblowers, those who had supported the efforts until seeing the ultimate direction of evil they were taking, came to the surface pointing the world towards what was happening; a setback Xander had foreseen. It was here that Xander, and a group of powerful world leaders initiated the first phase of their strategy. . . the release of enhanced bioweapons where opposition was at its heaviest. New diseases began to quickly take hold of the world, as the world found itself reeling in the unknown of such sickness and death, drowning out the noise of those who dared to blow the whistle. Their efforts of bringing the truth to light proved futile, as the sickened world increased their vocal demand for more and more vaccines. With a powerful hold over what was reported globally, the forum, under the instruction of Xander, began to use their influence to forcefully move the world to a stronger support of the need for newer vaccines, new testing, and greater understanding, while ostracizing anyone who vocally doubted, labeling them as conspiracy theorists and enemies. What served from this was a great division between those who were considered friends of the elite, and those who were considered opposition. It was here that the world's great divide between the wheat and the tares began, unknowingly preparing the tares who refused the truth, and instead blindly followed man's science, to one day soon receive Link18 with great excitement. And what came from such submission was a new, global authority, ushering in a never-before seen level of total control, that in its darkest corners was powerfully wielded from behind a curtain, by just one man. A man of lawlessness.

Chapter 19

AFTER THESE THINGS WERE in their foretold place, and before Xander was given his full authority as the Premier, Azul, knowing the signs of the times, left Xander with instructions to finish his work on Link18 in preparation of what was to come. With wickedness running rampant in the world, Azul brought his presence greater to the west, knowing their season was to come. As he stood a great distance from where he knew the destruction was to come from, he waited, until he heard the cry of command. From his place upon the shores, he witnessed the many souls instantly caught up from the world to meet their Christ in the clouds. Then, as foretold, the destruction imminently followed, as it was unleashed on those left behind. Though many would survive the first wave of devastation brought forth from the massive earthquakes at the New Madrid fault line, the second earthquake that followed along the western coastline of America, brought about a disaster that few would survive. . . the eruption of Yosemite into the western atmosphere. Suddenly, the western nations of North and South America, and the waters surrounding them, were instantly blanketed under a thick cloud of raining volcanic ash. The West, who had just days before, led the world to boast in the misplaced perception of an assumed peace and security, found themselves now reeling into extinction. After reveling in the west's destruction, Azul then returned to Xander, to prepare him for what was coming.

Days after the great disappearing, and the loss of the west, the United Nations activated emergency powers for regional control, under Xander's suggestion. Ten leaders were selected among them as regional authorities. When Xander met with the ten leaders, in their time of intense vulnerability, he presented new and powerful evidence that the events that were catastrophically sweeping the globe, were actually connected. Having worked with many leaders to have his satellites placed above each nation's atmosphere, he presented findings that shocked the leaders. Images Xander claimed to have captured, convincingly showed a large extraterrestrial force had attacked the planet. Xander explained how the images revealed what he believed, was the long-standing plan for their attack. With his deceitful words and manipulated images, Xander convinced the United Nations and their ten leaders, that it was the goal of the extra-terrestrial force to shock the world, by first abducting a large group from the Earth, comprised of what Xander deemed as "gullible Christians". He spoke passionately, that upon their abduction, the Christians had been easily fooled into thinking the event was the foretold Rapture of Christ's church. To further his point, Xander pointed to the infrastructure, military capabilities, and communications that were all significantly weakened as an immediate result of the disappearing. He set out to fully dismantle the Rapture theory in their minds, in whole. Xander pointed to the many famed pastors and preachers, along with a large contingent of their well-known mega-church congregations, remained throughout the world. Adding to his deception, his dear friend, His Holiness, had prepared a letter for the meeting, which Xander read aloud. Once the panel had been convinced that this was in fact, not the Rapture, as even some of them had early on begun to consider, Xander moved them to his next point—the destruction of a completely vulnerable west, that followed the disappearing.

Having a dense population of Christians, Xander argued, the powerful West was among the most instantly devastated by the sudden loss of those who were taken. He pointed to the sudden disappearance weakening their defense systems more than any other nation, which Xander pointed to, was the ultimate intent of the invading force. Xander proved his deceptions with the help of his powerful holographic images, presented as actual footage from his satellites. The ten regional governors believed Xander's words and the evidence he manufactured. They each stood convinced that once the nations of the west descended into chaos from the disappearing, the invading forces then amassed themselves over the west, detonating foreign weaponry, causing first, the earthquakes, before they then set sight toward the eruption of the super volcano, Yosemite. Xander deceived them all into believing these were not acts of God, rather that of a series of well-planned attacks, designed to remove one of the world's most powerful nations, with ease, leaving the rest of the world even more vulnerable. Xander then brought the ten even deeper into the deceptive lie. He brought with him military strategists from the east, that parroted his fabrication, having themselves been deceived by Xander. And in their deception, they too brought evidence from the satellites Xander had given them. The images from the east showed the invaders had been cloaked above Israel before the west's destruction, unbeknownst to their government. And as their shocked faces looked towards the screen, they watched as the video showed two seemingly extra-terrestrial beings being sent into the heart of Jerusalem, from the ship floating above it. The ten leaders looked at the images in horror, fearing that the terrifying beings that were responsible for the west's destruction, now walked dangerously among them.

As Xander closed his presentation, the leaders in attendance were greatly dismayed by the revelation of what was presented. Yet, before any of them could utter a word of response, the room went dark. Then, before them, the large screen above the conference room illuminated in a haunting red glow, before showing a clear image of a being not of human origin. Those in attendance, gasped at the sight of it.

Chapter 20

As THEY LOOKED UP at the screen with shock, many tried to quickly capture the image with their mobile device. Yet, as each tried, their device would electrify in their hand, and immediately cease from functioning. Chaos erupted among them, quickly. Xander, savoring the moment of his greatest deception yet, wore the look of one unphased. He stood boldly in the center of the room, looking around at the cowering leaders, who were crouching out of sight from the screen, for fear of the hideous being. As they hid themselves, Xander quickly placed his device on the control console, unbeknownst to any in the room. As he did, the being at once was heard speaking to them all. "You have been weighed in the balance and found wanting." The being said, chillingly. The attendees cowered in fear. Xander however, stood alone before the screen, with boldness. "What do you want from us?" he asked plainly, as the others hid themselves. "We want to cure you." The being replied. Xander gazed at the screen. "Cure us of what?" he asked. "Of yourselves." The being said, as its massive eyes widened further. The screen then immediately changed to show images of Earth's many wars, famines, pollution, and atrocities being committed. Among what was being displayed, were clear images of the world's history, as if they had been captured recently. "What is this?" one of the ten asked Xander, as he joined him before the screen. "I think it's proof they've been watching us for a while." Xander replied, as the images continued to play before them, showing in graphic detail, man's destruction of both Earth, and each other, over years of existence. The other leaders then joined together before the screen, standing with Xander, taking in the horrific images. Then, the screen once more returned to show the being. "You are a cancer. A plague. You do not deserve that which you have been given by us. We have now come to take it back from you before you destroy yourselves and other systems around you, with your negligence." The being said, garnering screams from some of the attendees. Xander looked around at the nervous faces of the room. He then looked up again to the screen. "Why is Israel so important to you that you've deployed two of your own there?" Xander asked. "We placed ourselves into your society and made ourselves into the image of your gods. In your weakness, you will accept us just as those we've taken from you." The being said. The ten leaders looked at the images in horror. "Religion. . . they plan to weaponize it." Xander turned, and whispered to them, before turning his eyes back to the screen. "Why tell us these things now? Why not just continue your conquest?" Xander asked. "So you will know you have no hope and therefor, will surrender. We are now walking among you. We will now close the skies, stop your rain, and unleash plague upon plague on your wretched race, until your reign of destruction has ended." The being said. Xander turned towards the ten leaders with a look of concern, before again turning his focus back to the screen. "Is there a way forward for us to peacefully coexist?" he asked. All who were in attendance, looked up at the screen in desperation. "Man cannot do what is required by we. It would take a god to do so. Therefor we cannot be appeased or challenged." The being said. Xander looked around the room once more seeing the visible fear in the eyes of the world's leaders. This was his moment to seize on the deception he had brought forward. Xander returned his gaze to the screen and smiled. "I think you underestimate us, friend." he said boldly, bringing a sudden shock over the room.

Chapter 21

THE BEING APPEARED TO gaze wickedly towards Xander. "Son of man. You are a fool. You cannot comprehend our power, nor can you stand against it. We know your weapons are primitive. We know you are divided. What is man that we should be mindful of him?" The being said tauntingly. Xander smiled. "You seem to know a great deal about us. I'll give you that. But do you know I've known about you for quite some time?" Xander asked, drawing a stunned silence from the room and the being. "Let me give you an example of what I mean. . . . I know about your seven warships you've stationed around our globe over each continent. It's hard to be in the business of global satellite deployment, and not discover the presence of life that extends beyond it. What I didn't know, was your intent. While you were planning what we now know was your attack, I was discovering your weaknesses and sharing it with the now deceased leaders of the west. Our only weakness was the west not sharing what I gave them, with the rest of the word, which to be fair, they paid for with their own lives when you destroyed them. But I know more than just these things, friend. I also know from which of your seven ships your personal transmission is currently coming from. What you may not know however, is that every one of those thousands of satellites I've deployed into Earth's atmosphere, was equipped with the advanced weaponry designed to exploit your own weaknesses. But we have no want among us to further this conflict. We want peace. We wish to live free, with the promise to your race, and every other race out there, that Earth will do better. However, we will not hesitate to defend ourselves." Xander said to the amazement of those in attendance. The being scowled at Xander. "You do not hold a single military advantage over we. If you did, you would have no problems proving it." He hissed. Xander looked around the room, as each of the leaders nodded approvingly to him. He looked back up to the screen, raised his device to it, and touched a series of buttons. Then he looked up from his device, towards the being. "Done, as you wish. You're on a ship currently hovering at thirty thousand feet, over Rome." Xander said. "Knowing where we are will not save you, now will it deter us." The being responded. Xander smiled. "Oh, to the contrary, knowing where you are is what helped me destroy you. I wonder how your other ships will fare at the sudden loss of their commander?" Xander replied, as the screen immediately went black. Xander brought up images from his satellites over Rome, showing massive explosions in the skies above, as the deceptive images showed the ship was completely incinerated. The room erupted with cheers. Suddenly, he quieted the room, pointing to his device. "We're being communicated with. Everyone, I'm going to put them through. Xander quieted the room, before again looking up to the screen, as the image of another being was shown. The being looked distraught. Xander smiled. "I assume you are the second in command. Let me tell you what happens now, number two, so we understand each other. I've given the world a deterrent against you. It's called Link18. I hereby order you out of our atmosphere, or I will further the attack and destroy your entire fleet with just a few pushes of a button. As for your two friends on the ground, please let them know their time among us is short. We'll find them. You can be assured as a race; we will do better with our world, going forward. But you have gravely misjudged us. We are free. And now, we are showing ourselves more powerful than you." Xander said tauntingly, as the leaders stood in awe of his authority. "We will not negotiate with you. You are not a god!" the being screamed. "Says who?" Xander replied, as the screen went black.

Chapter 22

WHEN THE SMOKE FROM the great deception had dissipated, the ten regional leaders at once joined together, giving Xander full authority over them, and their respective territories, under the promise of peace and security, and the hope that Link18 would be made available to all, connecting mankind together in great unity. With the full support and backing of the United Nations, in only an hour's time, Xander was named The Premier. The same day his authority was given to him, the images of the extra-terrestrial attack he claimed to have discovered, along with the images from its destruction of the west, were quickly made known to the world. After days of silence from the United Nations, after the disappearing and the West's destruction, the world finally received an answer to their question; what had come over the Earth. Weeks later, the United Nations excitedly announced to the world, Xander's role as the Premier. In his first public speech, he wooed the world with his strong words and promises of peace, and security. He ordered peace among the nations, establishing Kings over the Earth and her resources. He stood before the world, outlining a plan on how to move forward; one that emphasized green energy, peace through strength, and unifying the world's resources into one shared assortment, for the good of humanity. With the full support of the United Nations in those first days of his reign, he appealed to those countries outside of the United Nations, in lieu of the greater need, to join with him. The world marveled at his words and his courage. To commemorate a new and unified world,

the Premier's first act was to publicly declare a regionally supported peace treaty with Israel, in which a new temple was approved
to be built. Though seen as an olive leaf to the embattled nation,
as he shared with those in his innermost circle, this was merely a
means for him to hold greater visibility on the beings that were
deployed, and to control what he termed as *the deception of religion*, and the dangers it posed. Appearing in Jerusalem, in view of
the entire world, he and Israel's Prime Minister forged their treaty
together, unitedly ushering in a new era of peace. After appealing
to the heart of every man that remained in the world, as every
eye that beheld him marveled in his bravado, the Premier exited
the grounds that would serve as the location of Jerusalem's new
temple, to the cheers and fawning of the world who beheld him.
As the many flashes from the hundreds of cameras from those in
attendance, were snapped, suddenly, a shot rang out from among
them. The massive crowd screamed in horror, as onlookers rushed
away from the event. When the furied chaos came to a still, to
the horror of the world, the Premier, who had ridden out to the
world on his white horse to lead them, now laid lifeless on the
rocky ground of the would-be temple; a single gunshot wound to
his head.

Chapter 23

IMMEDIATELY AFTER THE ASSASSINATION of the Premier, the nations once more fell to anarchy. A powerful coalition of northern nations, with aspirations both religious and territorial, joined together against Israel. Seizing on the world's chaos, they set out with an immediate series of brutal attacks against a now-vulnerable Israeli nation, who had found themselves suddenly without allies. The actions of the invading forces immediately nullified the previous peace treaty, even before the ink of their signatures had dried. With the apparent death of the Premier, the coalition of nations knew this was their moment. Like a great fish being led by a hook, they were pulled to Israel, unified under their collective hatred of the Jews, under the orders of a single, powerful military leader, whom it was believed had orchestrated the attack on the Premier. Together, the massive force set out to seize control over the nation of Israel, and especially the natural gas pockets that had recently been discovered off its coast, which if captured, would serve as a powerful, world-altering acquisition. Amassed along the northern border of Israel, was one of the largest forces ever assembled by man. No nation came to the support of Israel in those days, as each were reserving their own resources among the destruction each had suffered, as they frantically braced for a shocking world conflict. After the second bloody incursion from the coalition was defeated, resulting in the deaths of twenty thousand Israelis, an appeal was made to Israel to surrender to the massive force. Yet Israel, standing more unified than ever, refused. The order was immediately given for the nations to increase the brutality of their attack. As Israel's iron Dome had been largely damaged, it was now left vulnerable from the sky. The leaders of Iran, a founding member of the northern coalition, who had been desperate to see Israel destroyed, were given the immediate authority to launch a targeted nuclear attack from their recently enriched uranium supply; a supply that had only been recently made possible, by the American treaty the middle east had signed days before the destruction of the west. The northern coalition, with their armies still amassed on the border, moved themselves back several miles, awaiting the nuclear illumination on Israel's western borders, as the powerful warhead launched from its silo. As it howled through the sky just above Israeli land, a sudden strong wind blew the large warhead off its course. The warhead spun wildly out of control, falling out of Israeli territory, and into neighboring Syria. Then suddenly, a giant nuclear cloud emerged from Damascus, as a large portion of the city was quickly engulfed by the massive nuclear blast. After the first cloud emerged, larger clouds of explosions from the great city erupted, as the nuclear weapons cache they had been secretly storing for the northern coalition, was detonated, leveling the entire city, and leaving it without survivors. The co-alition watched in horror, as the plumes of nuclear smoke could be seen from hundreds of miles away. In a moment of rage, the commander of the northern coalition ordered Turkey to launch its only two functioning nuclear missiles towards the center of Israel, away from the coast where the natural gas deposits were located. The warheads shot into the atmosphere with fury, and successfully penetrated the Iron Dome. Sirens blared throughout Israel as they watched in horror, the two warheads coming down towards them. Then, as they began to fall towards their target, two great winds suddenly emerged from the ground of Jerusalem. The warheads were miraculously thrusted northward by what appeared to be funnel clouds, well-beyond the outskirts of Israel. The leader of the northern coalition, who had presented himself magnanimously on the very battlefield the coalition forces stood on, watched with his troops in horror as suddenly, the two massive warheads appeared before them, falling over his army's massive forces, detonating instantly. The powerful blast scorched the entire northern coalition with fire, bringing every man and woman in attendance, as well as their great leader, to their sudden death.

The surrounding Nations of the middle east, who had chosen to sit idle with the rest of the world, cried out in desperation upon seeing the destruction of the great northern force. Fearing the escalation of war and the damage it would do to their own lands, all nations of the world, who had so willingly given their power over to the ten regional leaders, urged them to take greater hold of the nations once again, for the purpose of peace.

Chapter 24

XANDER STOOD ALONE IN the vast darkness that swept over him. Suddenly, a flash of crimson appeared before him. "Here stands he who is now before me." A voice said, from the flash, as it approached him to look at his head, where he had been mortally wounded. Xander peered deeply into the flash. "After everything that has happened, all that I've done, will you now show yourself to me?" Xander asked. The flash turned quickly, and before Xander, stood a large human-like figure, resembling that of a young man. Xander was taken aback by the sight. "You are *him*?" Xander asked in wonder, confused as he studied the beautiful face of the seemingly young man. "I am he, Xander.". Xander looked at the man in awe and watched as the towering being bent down before him to look him in his eyes. The man then reached out and touched Xander's wound, and suddenly, it was healed. Xander reached up to touch it for himself and was awe-struck. "I'm here to tell you what must now occur, as these things are written." The man said as he stood up, towering over Xander. "What must I do?" Xander replied as he too stood up, before kneeling before the man. "You left them as a man, Xander. But you will return with all my powers bestowed to you, by the secrets I have shared with you, through my servants who have successfully led the world to receive me. In your time of stillness, I have sent my servant to place a variation of the Link I've given you, to be placed into your body, as it will now heal you of your wound. With it, you will wake to my presence, as I will now take my place within you, just as my servant Azul, has fully taken his place in your servant, Darrell, the first to receive my mark. Together, we will now bring about my will on this world. All these things I have given to you, for you have bowed before me in worship. You will now rise from your wound. You will take your place as king amongst Kings and rule the world as I command. As I take hold of your Link and the Link of those who will surrender themselves to me, I will make them saints of a new order, unified for the single purpose of worship. You will now be my champion, who will pour out my wrath on this world and cleanse it of anyone who still holds to the first kingdom. You will take your place among the nations, strengthening your hold over them, and especially the wretched inhabitants of the woman, whom I hate. A place has been prepared for her. Yet, no matter. Many of her children will fall to me, as they have throughout time." The voice decried. "Yes, Lord." Xander replied. "And what of the two, or the ones foretold who are sealed?" Xander asked. "It is Moses and Elijah who he has chosen as his champions. Do not concern yourself with Moses and Elijah, for I will give them over to you. They will turn many away from us before their appointed time, as will those who rise from them. But the two prophets will fall to your hands by my power. And when they do, no further argument shall be had over their bodies. They will lie before the world, rotting. No angel will dare come to their rescue. Their demise will be as those who follow them. It must be ceremonial. You are to remove the heads of any who profess their loyalty to the other kingdom. You will leave the bodies of each where their rotting flesh will offend the indecisive. We must take as many of them as we can. We must rid the Earth of those who seek their savior, and in doing so refuse to bow their knee to me. You will be given the power to do great things, in my name. You, an image of man, but a god within you. You have fallen, Xander. You must now rise, Premier. I am with you now, and there shall be no end to our days. Xander, was then filled with the full power and authority of he who was speaking with him. Possessed fully by Satan himself, the Premier, having been on life support for six days since the assassination attempt, opened his eyes to the shock of those who were caring for him. And from that day forward, he and his master, were one.

Chapter 25

ASHEM WATCHED EAGERLY, TOWARDS the distant dunes. "They'll be here soon." Said Sif, who had joined him, handing him a metal cup filled with coffee. "Does she know?" he asked Ashem. Ashem took a small sip of his coffee, before shaking his head. "Do you intend to tell her?" Sif asked. Ashem again shook his head. Sif turned away from Ashem, with sadness. "I can't imagine the weight that will present for her, nor can I understand how heavy this is for you." He said, as he placed his hand on Ashem's shoulder. "The Lord's will be done. Tevah made that very clear. The 144,000 must move on, as one." Ashem said, stoically. As they stood together watching, suddenly, a large mass of robed figures appeared over the horizon.; behind them, a massive remnant of Jews who believed their words and followed them in the name of Christ. "There! Look how man the Lord brought to them!" Sif said, excitedly. Ashem smiled, though upon seeing them, his heart became heavy. As the group made their way through the narrow corridor of the dried river basin, all of Petra watched in joy as their heroes returned from their final mission. The men of the 144,000, each led back to Petra by the Spirit, rejoiced with those who awaited them. Maya ran to the front entrance as the men poured in. She waited eagerly to see her brother. She saw Tyrus enter. She at once, ran down to hug him. "My gosh, a year since I last saw you!" she said, as the two embraced. Tyrus was overjoyed in her presence. "Where's Abi?" Maya asked, as she looked around the many men. At once, Ashem came to where Tyrus and Maya were standing. Tyrus turned and hugged Ashem, as Maya looked over the large group trying to find her younger brother. "I'm grateful to see you, brother." Ashem said warmly. Yet as they embraced, Maya noticed Abi was not among those who had returned to Petra. Worried, she turned to Ashem and Tyrus. "Guys where is my brother?" she demanded. Tyrus turned to Maya. "He's in Jerusalem. Since the fall of new Babylon, the Beast has returned from Rome and is now leading all nations against Israel. The last of the remnant are being led to the rendezvous point by Abi where this group will meet them." Tyrus said. "Is he safe?" she asked, nervously. "Quite." Ashem quickly assured his wife. "Now rest up, dear friend. There is a long trek before the community tomorrow." Ashem said to Tyrus, as he left to speak with the others.

The next day, after the remnant had rested, Jessica came to Ashem. "It's done. Everything is finished and per your orders, it's live. We'll go ahead of you guys and report back as we see. Here's the control. Be careful with this, and remember, no more than 30 yards." She said as she handed a device to Ashem, before turning towards Maya. Maya stood up and hugged Jessica. "Be careful, Marine." She said in her toughened voice, as she wrapped her arms tightly around her friend. Jessica hugged Maya tightly. "I'll be fine. We have water and air conditioning in the truck. You guys just make sure you get there safely. Stay hydrated, missy!" She replied. Maya and Ashem watched Jessica and her team load into their vehicle, and set out north to the rendezvous point, where Abi was to meet them. As she watched them leave, Maya felt herself suddenly saddened. "Are you ok, love?" Ashem asked, seeing her visible concern. Maya turned toward Ashem and shrugged. "We've lost so much, it seems. Ima, my abba, Mash and Tevah, half of Jessica's team . . . I feel like it's been a lifetime since I last saw Abi. This is. . . hard. It's so much harder than I thought it would be. I just hope she'll be safe, Ash. I hope God will protect her. I just. . . I can't lose her too." She said, as she and Ashem hugged. Ashem, overcome by his wife's emotion, held her tightly. "Maya, we don't lose anyone. You must remember that. Once anyone among us is taken, we are at once, with Jesus, restored from this flesh." he said, before removing himself from her hold, and looking her in the eyes. "You understand this, right?" he asked. Maya was taken aback by his reaction. "I. . . I understand, Ash. I do. It's just hard, is all." Maya replied. Ashem pulled her close once more and hugged her. "My God, I know it is. Believe me, I know. But Maya, do not let another loss in your life take you from what God has deposited in you. You must guard the good deposit. Promise me this." Ashem insisted. Maya looked her husband in his eyes and smiled. "I promise." She said.

Chapter 26

"ALL CLEAR. YOU GUYS are a go. Now or never." Jessica spoke through the radio to the remnant at Petra, as she and her team had driven many miles out, putting eyes on the route the large caravan was soon to travel. As she did, Ashem stood before the mass that stood beyond the walls of Petra. Using Jessica's loudspeaker, he addressed them saying, "Now is our time. Brothers and sisters, you will travel as one. Whether you are new to our group, or have been among us from the beginning, you know that we depend on the Lord for all things. You will now enter the desert as the 144,000 who are with us, will protect us. Do not fear, friends. Fear nothing you see. You are going to call on the name of the Lord and He will hear you. His time has come.". The group roared aloud, as the caravan, surrounded by the 144,000, who stood proudly in their brown robes, were now ready to march north to meet with Abi in the foothills. They began to march from Petra, north. As the last of them emerged from Petra, suddenly, a large battalion emerged from the southern hills, moving quickly towards their direction. Ashem, seeing them pursuing quickly, ran with Maya ahead to where Sif was leading the group, to speak with him. "It's time. You know what to do." Ashem said, as he then turned to Maya. "You need to go ahead with Sif. I have to get the last of the caravan out. I'll be back to you soon." He said, as he hugged Maya, before disappearing into the massive crowd to go to the back where the remaining were just leaving Petra. The large battalion stormed the narrow corridor on their way to Petra. Suddenly, explosions erupted on both sides of the caravan, as the battalion, still a great distance from them, began firing mortars at their direction. The 144,000 however, by the power of the Holy Spirit, deterred the mortars and the fire of their explosions, resulting in no injuries for the fleeing remnant. At the back of the caravan, Ashem saw that all had left. He found Danny and Tomas, who were leading the last group and told them to make haste. Maya, walking with Sif in the first group, turned to see in the distance, Ashem standing next to the fortress, between the fleeing remnant and the pursuing horde of OWL soldiers. Maya looked at Siff, nervously. "What is he doing?" she asked, as she grabbed Sif's binoculars, and watched Ashem seemingly counting his steps from the fortress, before turning boldly towards the horde. Then, as she watched her husband stand boldly before them, she recalled that Tyrus and Abi had done the same thing before. She looked up to the sky, watching eagerly for an angel of the Lord to suddenly descend. But nothing happened. She then looked down to Ashem, as mortars began to explode around him, with him having drawn the battalion's fire towards himself.

Ashem, turning to see that the remnant was clear, looked up to Heaven. "You have appointed me for this time." He said, as his eyes then looked forward towards the battalion. He turned once more to look back to the remnant, smiling at them, before turning back to see OWL now just a few hundred feet from his position. Suddenly, gunfire erupted from them, as Ashem was struck in the chest. He fell to the ground and writhed in pain. Maya watched in horror as the Owl horde surrounded Ashem. "Oh my God, no! No! Where is Michael? What is happening?" she screamed frantically, as she watched, powerless to help her husband. The commander then brought his troops to a hold as he stepped out from their vehicle and surrounded Ashem. They watched as Ashem struggled to breathe. "Fa. . ." he tried to say, as the commander bent down to try and hear him. "Father. . ." Ashem said, his breath now fleeting. "He's finished." The commander said, as he stood from his position, drawing his pistol from his waist. Ashem looked up to heaven. "Father, into your hands I commend my spirit." He said, as the commander and his men laughed. The commander aimed his pistol towards Ashem's head, but just before he was to shoot, he saw Ashem was holding something. With his weapon still pointed towards Ashem, he reached down and pulled the device from Ashem's grip. The device, having a large green bLinking light, suddenly, clicked, as the light immediately flashed red. The commander looked down to Ashem's eyes, realizing he had removed a detonator from the dying man and in doing so, had unknowingly activated it. Ashem looked up and smiled. "It is just." He whispered, before closing his eyes and breathing his last breath. Suddenly, the fortress of Petra exploded, erupting fire from the deepest caverns inside. The massive blaze engulfed the owl battalion, killing every soldier in its wake.

Chapter 27

MAYA WATCHED IN HORROR as the flames of Petra blazed in the distance. The blast was so powerful, the entire startled remnant could feel the heat even from the many hundreds of yards they were standing away from it. The remnant watched with great sadness, as those of the 144,000 raised their hoods and sobbed as they walked beside them, mourning the loss of their friend, and leader. The next day, somberness accompanied them all, as they continued to march forward, toward the rendezvous point. From the moment the base erupted, Maya was inconsolable. Thrusted into the relentless sorrow of yet another loss, with Sif's reluctant permission, she separated herself from the group, choosing to walk alone, to mourn her fallen husband. She covered her head with Ashem's robe, as her tears dropped, burying into the sand next to her footprints. Then, when she was completely out of view from the remnant, she fell to her knees and cried aloud to God. "Haven't you taken enough from me?" she screamed, as she helplessly looked to Heaven. "Haven't I been faithful? How can you do these things? How can you let these things happen to your children? How could you take him from me, God? Answer me!" she demanded, as she cried, burying her head in her husband's robe; the calming scent of him still held by its fabric. Her heart was torn from her body as she whaled into the sand, she was laying in. "I choose to go no further for you. I can't do it anymore. I won't do it anymore. I have served you faithfully and you have taken my father, my mother, my friends, loved ones and now. . . you take my husband. Take me too,

Lord, please." She begged. "My pain is too great." She screamed, as she raised Ashem's robe to Heaven. After a few moments of silence, a great wind suddenly fell on Maya. Maya looked up to see the wind blowing from behind her. "Get up." A voice called out from the wind. "Get up, Maya. Join the others." The wind said. Maya sniffled, trying to find composure, while still steeped in her unrelenting agony. She looked around and saw she could no longer see anyone from the remnant, as she saw their tracks in the sand indicate they had all moved beyond the sandy hill, just over a hundred yards ahead of her. With what little strength she had remaining, she picked herself up, dusted herself off, and reluctantly set out over the hill, to catch up with the remnant. She continued to cry aloud, clutching Ashem's robe, writhing in her own suffering, as she marched exhaustedly towards her group. Thoughts of Ashem's words filled her heart, as she recalled his final encouraging words to her. . . "do not let another loss in your life take you from what God has deposited in you. You must guard the good deposit." She remembered him saying. The words rang cold in her mind as the truth began to fill her. It was then, she realized, Ashem had known all along he was going to sacrifice his own life, for the remnant. In her mind, she replayed his words from their time together, piecing together each clue he had given, while realizing he had never found the courage to tell her what was to come. She then recalled his words, "Maya, we don't lose anyone. You must remember that. Once anyone among us is taken, we are at once, with Him.". Yet peace itself was still hard to find in them, as Maya stood at the hill's ridge and made her way up to the top. As she walked ahead, her face still covered in tears, she came to the dune's peak and looked over to see the massive remnant beginning to encamp. Yet as she beheld them, she immediately noticed that the remnant had seemingly doubled in its size. In the distance, she saw Jessica's armored vehicle, as she and her team were handing out water to the remnant. Then, as she marveled at the collective sight of all before her, a figure suddenly emerged from the group, running quickly to her direction. She squinted out to see who it was and at once fell to her knees at the sight of him. It was Abi.

Chapter 28

THEIR REUNION WAS BITTERSWEET, as they hugged each other tightly, with tears pouring down from each. "I'm so sorry." Abi said as he gripped his sister tight. Maya looked at her brother with sadness. "Did you know it was going to happen, too?" she asked. Abi reluctantly nodded, and replied, "It was his calling. Tevah told him he would give his life for the remnant one day.". Maya's eyes closed, as she leaned into her brother's chest and whaled. "I don't understand any of this, Abi. Why didn't anyone tell me? My heart is shattered." She cried. Abi sat her down on the dune that overlooked the massive encampment. He gripped her hand tightly as he looked deep into her eyes, doing his best to resist his own tears from the news of his fallen friend, Ashem. "Maya, listen to me. Fight every instinct to be angry right now and just put your energy into listening. I have important words. . ." Abi said, drawing a sudden look of confusion from Maya. She wiped her face of her tears and listened to her brother, as he spoke. "Ashem knew his calling. He knew he was called to die for the remnant. He willingly took that on. He was in many ways, a man standing outside of the 144,000. He wasn't chosen to be one of us, despite all the time he spent with Tevah at the beginning of the Tribulation. Imagine the nobility of that. Walking with, and learning from Moses and Elijah, while bearing the full weight of leading the Lord's chosen, all while knowing you were not one of them by call, rather your service to God's kingdom would be martyrdom. . . I don't know a man among the 144,000 that holds the nobility of Ashem. Look around the encampment, and you'll see the mourning of everyone who ever knew and followed him. This, despite all of the pain, loss, and death we've each been called to witness. Ashem is greater than any man here. He was the voice that cried out from the wilderness to the 144,000. His humility was handpicked by God, through his servants. But all this aside Maya, you will see your husband again." Abi said, as his own tears started to flow. Maya sobbed, gently. "Why didn't he tell me, Abi?" she begged. Abi then smiled, drawing anger from Maya. "What can you possibly be smiling about right now?" she asked, angrily. "Maya, when Jesus revealed he was going to be crucified, it was Peter that replied that he would never let it happen to Him. Do you remember how Jesus responded to Peter's words?" Abi asked. Maya looked away and shook her head. "He said the words that I know would have killed me, if they were ever said to me by Christ. . . get behind me Satan." Abi said. Maya looked at Abi confused. "I don't understand how any of that applies to Ashem not telling me what every other person seemed to already know, Abi." Maya replied, frustratingly. Abi turned to his sister. "Look at me, Maya.". Maya was reluctant at first, but after his second request, she did so, staring her brother in his tear-filled eyes. "Had you known, you probably would've done exactly what Peter did in that instance. By your own words, you don't understand why God called this to happen. What do you think your response would be to Ashem's calling, had you known? He spared you of hearing from him, what Peter heard from Jesus, knowing you would have opposed his calling. Let me be the one to tell you, that when Ashem asked for my blessing for your hand, right after Ima was taken, he told me that you were the best thing that ever happened to him. You were a light from Christ Himself. But even his love for you couldn't compare to his love for Christ. He was willing to die, just as the Apostles all were. So, knowing you would try stand against it, he chose to keep his calling between us and Christ. I see the wisdom there. Rather than you both living together with darkness over you, he chose to hold the darkness from you. Maya, you are suffering now, no question. But your suffering now would be no different had you known before. Yet how much more would you have suffered during your time with Ashem, had you known the whole time? Whatever joy you held together, would've been destroyed knowing you would have to say goodbye one day. Would you have even enjoyed your time together, knowing his death was imminent? I'm sorry, Maya. Ashem was absolutely putting you first, by not telling you. You need to hear my words." Abi said, as he turned from his sister and looked out at the thousands upon thousands before them, just below the dune. Maya, moved to her heart, smiled to herself, before shaking her head at Abi's words. Abi looked at her confused. "What?" he asked. "It's just funny how with God, all things come full circle. It seems like only yesterday; Ash was giving me this same speech about you and Tyrus, and your calling." She said, warmly. Together, they sat with each other relishing one another's presence, as they looked out towards the massive remnant. After a moment of silence between them, she asked with a whimper. . . "He really did save them all, didn't he?". Abi smiled playfully and leaned into his big sister with a gentle nudge, saying, "Half of them. I mean. . . the other half I led here.". Maya smiled and hugged her brother, as the two watched the sun set over the encampment.

Chapter 29

THE LEADERS OF THE remnant, including Jessica and her team, sat together by the fire, with Abi, Sif, and many from the 144,000 that evening. They shared their stories of their many experiences in the world. They professed together, the name that had brought them out from the darkness that had come over the world, the name of Jesus Christ. With their vast collections of stories and testimonies, the night together gave them peace amidst their circumstances. When the topic of things to come had arisen, Abi stood up among the group to share the things the Lord had revealed to him through His spirit. With boldness in his words, the nearby crowds came closer, as a silence came over those within earshot. "I have stood in the presence of the Beast, three times now, with a message from the Lord. Each time, the Lord delivered me from death at the Beast's hand. The last time I was with him, it was to share the words that are on all of our hearts; soon the Lord will return. What comes for us, is tomorrow, the 144,000 will leave the encampment and make our way to the mount of olives, where we will very soon, be met by our Lord. We will sing the song he has placed in our hearts, believing in His glorious return. You, the remnant of Israel, will stay here and wait. A tremendous war will begin soon. The Kings of the East have come here with a massive force and will meet the Premier in the valley, for the battle of Armageddon. This will certainly spill over to this location. Amidst the bloodshed, they will come for you, as both see you as the greater threat. But do not be afraid. What gave us power to protect you to this point, will come upon you when you, the remnant, lift your voices to Heaven as one, and cry aloud for the return of Yeshua, the savior of Israel. After this, the sign will appear, and the nations will mourn, like children who destroyed their parent's home while they were away. Their mourning will not be one of repentance though, as they have taken Satan's mark and are now like unreasoning animals, filled with the wickedness of Hell. Brothers and sisters, hear me. You will see the culmination of everything that has ever been spoken of by the prophets. You will see it. We don't know the exact time, or if any of us will be called to death. What we do know, is He who has promised to deliver us from this, is faithful. He will surely do it." Abi said to the cheers of the encampment. Maya beamed with pride, seeing the maturation of her once immature little brother. She marveled as she watched him give comfort to all those around him.

As each had begun to rest in their makeshift tents and beds, Abi joined Jessica and Maya at their fire. "No rest for you, ladies?" he asked as he sat down with them. Both women shook their heads. "She never sleeps." Maya joked, pointing to Jessica, whose eyes continued to look up, watching over the vast horizon for any signs of OWL. She looked at Maya and smiled, sarcastically. Abi poked at the fire, to stoke the flames more. "I get it. You've seen a lot." Abi said. "Not as much as you have though." Jessica replied, as her eyes returned to the fire. "What's it like out there? I noticed no one had the guts to ask you that, aside from what was happening in Jerusalem." She said. As she spoke, a vast array of explosions in the distant night sky could be suddenly heard from a great distance away. The war between the Premier and the Kings of the East, had begun.

Chapter 30

"It's mostly dark, according to the ones who came to Israel this year. Most of those that the Lord placed into my care, were left letters at the Rapture, by their loved ones, urging them to find a way to Israel, knowing it was the place Christ said He would return. They've seen things out there, that we have not seen, from here. That's the truth. From what I've gathered, the oceans have no life in them anymore. There are more rivers of blood than rivers of water. The few animals that remain or almost zombie like from the chemical warfare that's been released over the globe. The west is nothing more than an ash heap, still. The sun doesn't shine in Europe. They're in an almost eternal state of overcast. The East is in tatters. There's little to no food. No water. No peace. My spirit confirms that billions have perished to this point. I can only imagine what's going through the minds of those who took the mark and are now understanding how much they were deceived. Truth be told, in our encounters with them, they don't even seem human anymore, apart from their emotions. You should see them. They look like people crying out in an abyss of themselves, desperate to escape their own fate, realizing having taken his mark, they've doomed themselves. But truth be told, there's more Satan in them, then the person they were before they took the mark. It's heartbreaking. I can't imagine many undecideds remain. But, if they do, the Holy Spirit will urge them here. Every day, more and more baskets are filled with the heads of our brothers and sisters. The last time I spoke with the Premier, that Beast boasted about it to my face. My only comfort was to remind him that those he's killed will be those who arrive at his destruction." Abi said, with sadness. "Do you think he believes the ending of the Bible?" Jessica asked. "I don't know what he believes. I know whatever it is, it's Satan that believes it. I don't think a man rose, after the assassination, truth be told. When I look into his eyes, I feel Satan looking back at me, with pure hatred for my existence. He knew about Ima. He knew about Abba's faith, too. I think whatever man he was before that day, is long gone. Now, he's like all mark bearers. Satan in the flesh. But, to your question, I think Satan's whole purpose in life was to test God's sovereignty. To look upon perfection and try to find its cracks. Mash-Pekh told me that. He told me that in matters of Satan, to picture a child that had one day, disobeyed his father. Instead of the story of the prodigal, where the son comes confessing his wrong to his father and working together to fix it, instead Satan gave way to his pride, and made a life out of hurting his father. The ultimate projection. Do wrong and when the consequences come, blame the judge for it. That's what he did. And when his father responded by creating life that would replace him and those he deceived, Satan declared war on those who were chosen. He hates us. He hates what we represent. We stand to gain everything he and his followers lost. I don't know what he tells himself now that his father's words are coming to light. I don't know how he reconciles all this coming to a head. I just know his time is almost finished, for now." Abi said, as he continued to poke at the fire. "What do you mean, for now?" Jessica asked, curiously. "The 1000-year reign." Maya replied. Abi smiled at her, proudly. "What? I listen. You can't be married to someone life Ashem and not hear the things he said." She joked. Jessica turned to Abi. "Right! The 1000-year reign. Refresh me on that. . .", she asked. Abi, still poking into the fire, replied saying, "Christ will finish the Beast and his false prophet. They get thrown into the lake, instantly. But Satan himself will be bound for 1000 years, as Christ returns to reign on Earth. His rule. His government. His peace. The nations will thrive. But. . . after those 1000 years, Satan will be released, and he will again make war against the kingdom. Then he will be captured, bound, and destroyed. We don't fully know why the 1000 years needs to happen, or everything that ultimately happens during this time. Whether it's a second chance for those who were deceived, to come to Christ, or what. There's quite a bite that we won't know until He comes to establish His kingdom and reveals the mystery of God.". "Ugh, I wish it would just all end tomorrow." Jessica said, as she too looked into the fire. "It might." Abi replied.

Chapter 31

THE NEXT MORNING, THE remnant awoke to see the 144,000 had somehow left them in the middle of the night. Without so much as a sound, as if carried by the spirit, they had set out unbeknownst to most of the remnant, for the Mount of Olives. Seeing that they were gone, many in the remnant gave way to nervousness, fearing their sudden loss of protection. The day they were brought together, the massive remnant had been divided into twenty groups, with each group selecting a leader from amongst them. The chosen remnant leaders from each group came to Jessica's tent, where she and Maya were, seeking their instruction, as Maya and Jessica found themselves suddenly thrusted into leadership roles. Maya, taking hold of everything Ashem had himself demonstrated to her, ordered calm from the group, explaining to them that as she understood, there would still come persecution. "Go out to your people and to your captains and spread the word. Each of you must remind them who they serve. This is not a time of panic. Even if all of us are called into death, we know, to death we go. I don't know what will come over that hill, or when it will come. I can tell you that last night, we heard the war from Jerusalem began, between the Beast and the Eastern Kings. It's started. You all slept through that without worry. Why do you worry now? Be excited that the battle has begun. Look up! Challenge your people to do so. Don't you see? This means our Lord will soon return. Keep your faith there. You're leaders. Your faith will be your people's faith. Praise through it all, even unto death! Now go and serve your people with those words!" Maya said, as the leaders each returned to their massive groups, doing their best to ensure peace was maintained among them. As the remnant braced itself for the unknown, more and more scattered people from the north, fleeing war-ravaged Israel, made their way to their location, having been led by the spirit. They were met with welcoming arms, praising the name of Jesus for leading them to their location. As the numbers grew through-out the day, so did the sounds of war. Yet Maya, having found her own strength, refused to allow anyone in her midst to worry. As night fell once more on their location, the remnant sat together, singing songs, and rejoicing together at the thought of a returning Christ. Jessica and Maya sat together and were joined by Justin and Phillipe'. "I guess it won't end today." Jessica said to them. Maya nodded, as her eyes were now the ones looking across the vastness of the dark dunes. "Not today." She replied.

The next morning, the remnant awoke to a startling cry. Maya opened her eyes and at once, turned towards Jessica, who also had been awakened by it. Both women ran from their tent to see what was happening. In the distance, at the most northern point of the remnant, the men and woman were running south towards Maya and Jessica's location. Jessica ran into the ten and pulled from it her binoculars, as she immediately looked over the dunes at the northern location. There, she saw them. The Premier's army had amassed itself together, as it barreled towards them all. Jessica dropped her binoculars at the sight of the massive horde. "My God, be with us." She said, as she bent down and retrieved the binoculars, before then handing them over to Maya. Maya gasped at the sight. Then, just before the northern part of the remnant, missiles began to strike the furthest point of their location, de-stroying those who were fleeing Israel, in their attempts to join the remnant. "It's starting!" Maya yelled, as Jessica turned from her and ordered Phillipe' to the truck for their weapons. "We'll hold them off." Jessica insisted. As she turned to leave, she no-ticed Maya's hand grabbing her arm. "No. You can't." Maya said, with command in her eyes. Jessica, confused, nudged herself free from Maya and moved quickly to the trucks. Maya chased after her, pleading. "Jessica, this is pointless. This won't do anything but get you killed. You won't stop them. You won't even slow them. You have to stay here. We must stay together, in our faith. This is not the time to rely on ourselves. Please!" she pleaded. Jessica, paused for a moment. She looked up to where her team were loading their weapons, knowing they had been willing and ready to give their lives. She looked back to Maya, who watched her in desperation. "Please." Maya whispered, beggingly. Jessica shook her head and looked back to her team. "Put them down." She said, drawing the immediate ire of Justin. "What?" he asked, shocked by her orders. "We have to put them down. We can't live by our own sword anymore." She said, as Maya exhaled with relief. Justin looked up to see the Premier's forces were continuing to strike the northern most point, as his strikes seemed intent on pushing the northern camps to the south. Then, out of nowhere, a sudden wall of fire erupted from behind the southern location, just a few hundred yards from their tent, trapping them from escaping south, as several Eastern kingdom fighter jets screamed over their position. The group looked and saw the massive battalions emerging from behind them, as the Kings of the east, began their own engagement. "They're herding us, Jess. They're both drawing us to the center of the dunes, like cattle for the slaughter. There's nowhere to escape to. We're sitting ducks here!" Justin pleaded, as he cocked his machine gun, eager to return fire. "If you fire a single shot, you will lose the faith of this entire remnant." She yelled to him. "All of you, put down your weapons, now!" she ordered. The group looked at each other, confused. Jessica sighed. "Guys. . ." she said, pleadingly. "Jesus won't come without our faith placed solely in Him. Who do you serve? Your guns, or your God?" she asked them, plainly. At once they looked at each other. Then, each of those who remained of Jessica's team, threw their weapons to the ground. They all joined Maya and Jessica at the top of the ridge where the remnant was being pushed towards. Then, even more explosions were heard from behind them. Jessica turned to see the Kings of the east advancing towards them, their massive infantry now closing in on their position.

Chapter 32

"We have them, Lord. They are completely cut off from retreat. Our enemies have cut them off." Darrell said, as he and the Premier watched eagerly, as the remnant stood trapped between the two massive forces who were continuing to fire at each other. "Don't waste good artillery on that pathetic group." The Premier ordered to his general, referring to the remnant. "Sir?", the general replied. "Let their lives be nothing more than the collateral in my war with Phi and the other Kings." He said. The general nodded, as he ordered his forces to advance. Artillery began to fire over the remnant as they quickly found themselves in the crosshairs of the two opposing forces. As the scattered debris of artillery fell by their location, the massive remnant joined together, huddling below the dunes, and pleaded with God for His intervention. The remnant prayed, giving unified worship to the God of Israel, and at last, His son, their Savior. All of Israel, those who remained unmarked, praised the name of Jesus, begging Him to now deliver them from the wrath of the Beast. As the explosions around them sounded, suddenly, they stopped. Maya, huddled together with thousands, upon thousands of frightened saints, excitedly looked up, yet as she did, she again saw nothing. Then, from over the hills, a sound began to emerge from hundreds of miles away. A song echoed out from the desert sky. Jessica and Maya looked at each other, their eyes widened. It was being sung from the mount, by the 144,000. They were singing the song that only they had known, and the song was filling all of Israel. Maya and Jessica screamed to the others what the song was and told them to hold their faith, as their words echoed out to the entire remnant, as they too, began to praise Jesus once more. All who were around them, joined in their praise, as they too miraculously heard the song of the 144,000. The Premier, standing still many hundreds of yards away from the remnant, scowled at the noise. He looked at Darrell in disgust. "Send the jets to the mount, now!" he ordered. Darrell nodded and gave the order. The Premier looked down towards his General. "General Hasheem, I've changed my mind. I want you to focus all your fire on the remnant now. They spit in my face with their blasphemies. Wipe their faces from their bodies and let them burn." He ordered. The General nodded, as he gave the order. With hundreds of thousands gathered into the shallowest parts of the dunes, they huddled together, continuing to praise the name of Jesus, as they cried out, "Yeshua, return!". Their praises grew louder and louder. As they praised, they soon heard the howling sounds of many missiles, as they were now hurling towards them, at rapid speed. "They're firing at us, now. Hold together and lift your voices up!" Maya screamed out loud from the center of the remnant, as her words were immediately echoed out by those nearby. Maya grabbed Jessica's hand, as the two held on to each other, as they shouted to the Lord with all their might. Suddenly, the missiles detonated above them.

"What happened?" the Premier yelled to his general, before turning a hardened glare to him. "I . . . I don't know, sir." The General replied, before ordering another strike. In the distance, the sound of the 144,000 and their song, still echoed throughout the hills, continuing to echo throughout the entire nation of Israel. "Why am I still listening to that?" the Premier screamed to Darrell. Darrell at once, radioed to the air battalion, but there was no response. He looked up nervously to the Premier. "I can't get them on the com." He said. The Premier scowled. Then suddenly, a massive eruption stormed over the skies, as both armies were suddenly blinded by a great and brilliant light. As all together beheld it, the entire sky seemed to be now separated in two. The Premier and his forces looked up, as did the Kings of the east. In the center, where the sky had divided, stood a massive glowing cross that could be seen all throughout Israel, and the world. "What is that thing?" General Hasheem screamed in terror, in earshot of his men who were all equally dismayed by its illuminating sight. The Premier looked up, and instantly, he too was afraid. Across from their position, the remnant looked up, in awe, as they watched a stunning glow emit from behind the cross. Then, every eye that dared look up, saw a brilliantly illuminated figure then emerge from the startling light of the cross. The figure was glowing more powerfully than the radiant cross, and its aura, as they stepped forward from the cross. "What is that? It. . . It looks to be a man, riding a horse!" the generals of Phi's armies began to shout in fear, as terror consumed the forces. Without orders, they instantly turned their weapons upward, in fear of what was coming.

Chapter 33

THE PREMIER STOOD NEARLY frozen at the sight of him, as he looked up to the sky helplessly. "Shoot! Shoot Him down!" he ordered of his battalion. The firepower from his entire army, combined with the Kings of the East, filled the entire sky, but as it was with the missile fired towards the remnant, all their artillery turned to immediate ash. Then, the glowing figure who was riding the horse moved forward from the glowing cross. The remnant continued to look up in awe. As they watched the fulfillment of what they had been promised was to come, their eyes all filled with tears. There, before them all, was Jesus, sitting ready on His glorious horse. He had returned to them. His eyes were like flames. The surrounding armies screamed in terror as they saw Him. The Premier, shaken to his core, ordered his generals to fire once more at Him. But, as he gave the command, Jesus looked instantly towards him, where he and Darrell were standing with the generals of their armies, His flaming eyes burning with rage. Then, Jesus spoke with the sound of thunder. . . "Peace be still.". At once Satan and his servant, Azul, were both thrown from Xander and Darrell's bodies, as the two men looked on in horror. The generals, and the soldiers who saw what Jesus's words had done to their leader, screamed, as they ran from their position, seeking to be hidden from Jesus. The remnant watched as Jesus rode his horse slowly above them, looking down at them and rejoicing at their sight. Jesus smiled at them, as His peace filled their hearts. It was then the remnant knew; their suffering was over. As Jesus rode out from the cross, more on horseback followed Him. Moses and Elijah, who too, were on horseback, appeared. Then emerged Peter. Then John and James. Then, Paul and the rest of the Apostles, who all were on horseback, as their Savior was. Behind them emerged David, Noah, Job, Amos, Zachariah, John the Baptist, Elisha, Joshua, Mary, and every saint and prophet that was ever faithful to the Lord. Mounted as soldiers prepared for war, they sat on their radiant white horses, hovering over the fleeing hordes watching the armies below them trying to escape. President Phi looked around desperately. "Hide me! Hide me from His wrath!" he screamed to his fleeing soldiers. Yet as he was screaming, Jesus drew his sword and cried aloud. As He did, all of those who were wicked, fell, as each was instantly stricken by the power of His cry, as if His sword had struck them. As the faithful from Heaven stood together, angels then emerged from the cross, hovering around them all, singing. Then, a voice from the sky declared. . . . "Come gather for the great supper of the Lord. To eat the flesh of Kings, the flesh of captains, the flesh of mighty men, the flesh of horses and their riders, and the flesh of all men, both free and slave, both small and great.". As the enemies of the world lay dying before them all, they watched as Gabriel, who had spoken the words, flew over them. Gabriel screamed out in thunder over the horizon, as the whole sky soon filled with birds of the air. As the birds assembled, they at once flew down to engorge themselves on the flesh of the wicked. And with their last wicked stare, the men who had refused Him, saw that even the birds of the sky surrender to His authority. And it was so, that the birds of the sky, coming to feed on their flesh, was the last any of them would see. Then, two angels at once, flew from their position and took hold of Xander and Darrell, who pleaded with them for mercy. Yet, for these two, no mercy was found. The Lord looked on the fallen hordes of wicked men, those who had been responsible for the blood of His tribulation Saints, and He spoke over their corpses with the roar of many lions, saying, "It is finished.". The remnant screamed in their praises. They were delivered. Then, suddenly, a great wind lifted the entire remnant, as well as all of those from around the world who too, had longed for Christ's return, refusing the mark of the Beast. They were all lifted together from their places and carried to the center of what remained of Jerusalem. Thousands upon thousands stood together in Jerusalem, where they saw the 144,000 waiting on the mount of olives, rejoicing as Jesus' rode to them on his brilliant white horse. As Jesus stepped down from is horse, the moment his foot touched it, the entire mountain was then split into two, separating it and creating a valley between the mountains, signifying God's judgement had come. As the faithful stood in awe, watching these things, then, Michael descended from the great cross in the sky, into the center of the faithful, holding in his hands a large key. The remnant cheered his arrival, as the armies of Heaven watched him then take hold of Satan, walking him forcefully toward Jesus. As he walked Satan through the crowd of the faithful, they marveled at the sight of him. He appeared to them, as a child, harmless in his nature. "This is him? This is the one who accused our brothers?" they each said to each other, shocked at his harmless appearance. Satan looked around at them all and wept, bitterly. Michael, having brought the deceiver before Him, then looked up to the mountain at Jesus and waited. Then, Moses and Elijah took hold of Xander and Darrell, as each had been captured. In the middle of the mount of olives, two holes in the earth opened; one a black pit of nothingness, and the other, a lake of fire. Elijah took immediate hold of Darrell and threw him into the lake, as he was consumed by its excruciating fire. The remnant of Christ cheered his demise. Then, they watched as Moses took forceful hold of Xander and brought him to the lake. Xander begged Moses not to cast him into it, but Moses seized him tightly and peered into his wicked eyes. "It is just!" he screamed, as he then threw him in to the ceaseless lake, to burn for eternity. The faithful, with many who he had himself killed, watched as Xander writhed in the agonizing pain of the ceaseless fire of the lake. Then, Michael walked up to where Moses and Elijah were standing, dragging Satan by his foot, as he clawed at the ground, to try and escape. Michael stood Satan before where Christ was standing with His elect on the mountain. He looked at Satan and shook his head. "Now the Lord will rebuke you." He said, as he forcefully turned Satan to face Jesus.

Chapter 34

JESUS, LOOKED DOWN AT him, sadly. He was then joined by Raphael, Uriel, and Gabriel, as each looked upon the sad state of their fallen brother. Jesus then nodded to Michael, and without hesitation, Michael cast Satan into the darkness of the pit that had no bottom, where he would remain for 1000 agonizing years of powerless torment. Then Michael looked up to Christ and declared to all, "The kingdom of our Lord has come." He said, as everyone in attendance, bowed before Christ. The saints, all standing together, united as one in the great city that was to be rebuilt soon after, rejoiced together as they praised Him, their king and Savior.

In the moments that followed, those who had remained alive in that time, hugged each other. Maya held Jessica tightly. "We made it! We made, Jess!" she said, as they both watched Angels fly over them, in the skies above Israel, led by Jacob and his sons, who at once began to restore their namesake. As the two women were hugging, a voice from behind them called out. . . "Maya. . .". Maya turned and there before her, was Ashem, restored in his new, glorious body. Maya fell at once before him, overwhelmed by the sight of her fallen husband. Ashem reached down and grabbed her, lifting her from the ground and holding her in his arms. "I told you. You don't lose anyone." He said as she cried with joy in his arms. She looked over to where she knew Jessica was standing, and saw her suddenly hugging two restored women, crying in their arms as Maya was, in Ashem's. The two locked eyes on each other, as they rejoiced in the return of those they lost, whether in the Rapture, or the Tribulation. As their eyes locked, they knew then that all they had endured, was finished. They would no longer be subject to death, or pain. They would never lose anyone again that they loved. It was over. They cried together, Maya in the arms of Ashem, and Jessica in the arms of her mother, and sister. Ashem then set Maya down, took his finger and wiped her tears. "Save them. You'll need them." he said to her confusion. He then pointed behind her. As she turned, there behind her stood Ima, also restored to her youth. Ima shook with joy at the sight of her daughter who she knew, had endured so much without her. And just a few feet from her mother, standing too, was her father, restored and in the glory of the Lord. Maya's eyes widened and she shouted towards them. She ran into her parent's arms and screamed with joy. "But how? Why? When did you come to Christ, Abba?" she screamed in disbelief while frantically hugging both of her restored parents. "He made His appeal to me just before, because of the suffering you would be called into, Maya." Her father said. "Thank you for enduring it, all." He added, as Maya wept loudly in his arms. Maya stood amazed as she looked into the eyes of her parents. She realized how much her suffering was worth the price she paid, when she understood that it all worked together for the good of God's kingdom. As she hugged them both, she looked up and saw Jesus in the distance, standing with his arm on Abi's shoulder, as both were watching them, smiling at their reunion. She whispered out to him only three words. . . "Thank you, Jesus.". Jesus smiled. "Your welcome, my child." He said. And from the mountain he looked out unto the vastness of his saints who were reunited as one, together. He smiled at them and raised His hands over them. And with His mighty voice, he cried out to them all. . . "Well done, good and faithful servants. Come and share your master's happiness.".

And from that day forward, His kingdom reigned without end. Every crying eye was wiped of its tears by His own hands. And those heroes of the faith, both old and new, stood together as one; the body of Christ fulfilled.

Are you **saved**?

If you can't remember the date,
If you can't remember the time,
If you can't remember the moment,

Stop everything and pray...

"Lord Jesus, I believe you are the Son of God. That you died on the cross to give me salvation. In doing this, you have delivered me from death. I choose now to turn from my old, sinful ways and every part of my life that doesn't align with your word. I choose you. I give myself to YOU, Lord. Lead me from this day, forward."

May the Lord welcome and keep you.

God bless you!

Epilogue

IMAGINE ONE DAY, COMING to the understanding that what's been written here in this book, will one day take its place in our world. Imagine waking from the horrors of this book to find that by God's grace alone, you still have time to come to Him and thus, be saved from the pages I was led to write. What will you do with such a gift?

www.ingramcontent.com/pod-product-compliance
Lightning Source LLC
Chambersburg PA
CBHW072009170626
46813CB00005B/2086